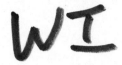
WI

THOUGH THE WINDS BLOW

IW

THOUGH THE
WINDS BLOW

Judith Blake Schaefer

To order additional copies of this book, contact:
Xlibris Corporation
1-888-795-4274
www.Xlibris.com
Orders@Xlibris.com
28494

In memory of Ted Jr. and Ted Blake Schaefer

CONTENTS

Preface

I wrote *Though the Winds Blow* because the organizing event of this novel—the death in 1953 of Glen Waibel, a close family friend and a prominent merchant in Huron, South Dakota—significantly impacted my life. Many years later I revisited this unsolved mystery by rereading newspaper clippings and letters written that winter. I've changed the names of people involved and added a fictitious boyfriend. In fact, the last half of the novel is fiction. Although I've resolved the mystery in the novel, it was never solved in real life.

Acknowledgments

I'd like to thank Steve and Jodi Schaefer for their many forms of support. Sheldon White, Chris Smith, Louise Corman, Paule Daum, Philip Gray, Alexandra and Ed Buturla, Suzanne Millar, Lauren Jagurnauth, Milt Budoff, and Harlan Blake provided many helpful comments and criticisms. Special thanks to Robin Stratton, my editor. Without her, this novel would never have been completed.

Prologue

South Dakota, 1998

Marty listened to the wind whistling eerily through the TV rotor on the roof, evoking spirits of her past. She heard her father reciting: *"The North wind shall blow and we shall have snow and what will Robin Redbreast do then, poor thing. He'll hide in Don Wagner's barn."* She was little, standing on a chair looking out the kitchen window toward the barn at the back of the neighbor's yard, a structure barely visible through the swirling snow.

In summer the dust storms—more wind, howling and whipping up the earth into black clouds. Her mother's voice now: *"Hurry into the house. Close the windows."* And the tornado. Her father's voice again: *"Stay down. Keep low."* They had dropped into a ditch along the road near the lake cottage in fear the funnel would touch down nearby.

One April, walking home from school, the sweet smell of lilacs wafting in the gentle spring breeze. Wally's voice: *"Marty, let's pick some lilacs for your mom."*

Years later, Rich's voice: *"Put on your life jacket and stay in the cabin."* Their small sloop, blown about on Lake Michigan by an

1

unpredicted storm; only the sea anchor kept the boat heading into the wind, kept it from capsizing.

Richard's voice again, *"Look at the telltales. We've got a breeze."* Welcome words. Welcome wind! No longer becalmed on Lake Michigan after dark.

All so long ago. How did she come to be here with these spirits on this day in this place?

Chapter One

South Dakota, 1953

Where is He?

When the phone rang, CB said, "I'll get it, Ellen." He got up from the kitchen table, walked into the dining room and took the receiver off the hook of the black wall phone. "Hello?"

"CB, this is Lars Erickson. Is Don Wagner there?"

"No. Why?"

"He was supposed to meet me at 7:00 to order hardware for the store. It's 7:30 and he hasn't shown up. I know he eats dinner with you quite often."

"It's not like Don to be late. Did you call his house?"

"I did. No answer there or at the store."

"I'll make a few calls. See if I can find him."

"Thanks, CB. I didn't know who else to call. I'll wait here at the Daum. We usually meet in the lobby."

Ellen was standing in the doorway when he hung up. "Anything wrong, Charles?"

"I don't know. Don's late for his appointment with Erickson. Where do you think he'd be having dinner tonight?"

"Bob Meyer's, maybe?"

"I'll call his house first."

Three unsuccessful phone calls later, Ellen said, "Charles, let's go to his house. Maybe he fell or had a stroke."

"Okay, let's go."

They said little as they drove through the quiet town—a town silenced by a near blizzard the night before. A thick blanket of snow glistened in the glow of streetlights. "It's a winter wonderland." Ellen tried to conceal her anxiety as they approached Don's house—a brick 1930s Tudor she always admired. "The house is dark."

"Don may be in the back." CB walked up to the front door, rang the bell, looked around, and returned to the car. "He's not answering. Let's go to the hotel. He's probably with Erickson by now."

"The car must be in the garage, Charles. The driveway hasn't been shoveled and there aren't any tracks."

"He'd take the truck in this weather. I'd check the other garage, but we might get stuck in a snow drift on the side street."

Bob Meyer and Lars Erickson, waiting near a phone booth when Ellen and CB entered the hotel lobby, turned to greet them.

"He hasn't shown up?" CB knew the answer before he asked the question.

"No."

"Could there be any mistake about the time?"

"Not likely. He confirmed the time and place this afternoon."

CB turned to his wife. "We'd better go back to the house. He must have had an accident." His voice reflected his growing concern.

"I'll go with you," Meyer said. "I've been worried ever since you called."

"Alright. Let's take Ellen home first in case there's a call there."

"I'll stay here a while longer," Erickson said. "Call me when you know something."

After they dropped off Ellen, Meyer lit a cigarette. "Don called the store three times today. First he called to say he'd be coming in late. Something about a business deal he was working on."

"I was surprised he wasn't in the store this morning when I dropped in, so I called his house. He always works from 8:00 to 6:00, and he never misses a day, except Sunday."

"Right. The second time he called, he asked me to come to the house," Meyer continued. "When I got there, he asked me to go to the bank and get $9,500 in 50 and 100 dollar bills."

"What? Why?"

"I don't know. He said he'd explain later."

"Well, I smell a rat. Was anyone in the house with him?"

Meyer hesitated. "I don't know. He didn't invite me in when he gave me the instructions or when I came back with the money. I stayed on the front stoop. He was in the doorway. I didn't hear or see anyone else."

"The third phone call?"

"To confirm the appointment with Erickson."

CB stopped in front of the house. "I'm going in this time if I have to break the door down."

Meyer followed him up the front steps. The front door opened easily. CB found the light switch in the entrance hall and entered the living room. He walked quickly through the dining room and kitchen. Everything seemed in order. "I'm going upstairs, Bob." He didn't wait for Meyer, still standing in the hallway, to respond.

Halfway up the stairs CB saw light from Don's bedroom at the head of the stairs and knew in his gut Don would be there. But nothing could prepare him for the quiet shape—his best friend—lying across the blood soaked bed, a gun in his right hand. Stunned, he stood momentarily frozen in the doorway. He did not go into the room. No reason. Don was dead. As he turned to go down the stairs to call the coroner and the police, he saw a photograph of his own two daughters, Marty and Liz, on the dresser next to the bed.

Chapter Two

Chicago, 1953

Coming to Grips

When the phone's ringing penetrated her sleep, Marty sat up quickly, alert, foreboding mingled with surprise. Who would be calling so early on a Sunday? Or was it still Saturday? None of her Chicago friends would phone in the middle of the night. She stumbled toward the kitchen, not stopping to find a light switch, intent on reaching the phone.

"Sorry to call so early, Marty, but I've been up most of the night. I have terrible news."

"What's happened, Liz? Are Mom and Dad alright?"

"They're okay. It's Don. He died last night."

Marty, her hands shaking, fumbled for the light switch. "Don? Dead? How?"

"Apparently, he shot himself in the head. Mom said he left a suicide note for Dad."

"My God, Liz." Marty found the switch, but the light did not dispel the nightmare.

"I know. Mom also said Dad thinks he might have been murdered."

"Murdered? Why?"

"It just happened last night, Marty, only a few hours before Mom called, so I guess nobody really knows much yet."

"Liz, we need to get out there. They must be devastated, especially Dad."

"Yes. I'll make reservations for us and get back to you."

"Okay. Thanks."

Images, thoughts, memories, questions. Marty paced from one end of her small basement apartment to the other. Why would Don kill himself? This man she'd known all her life, a kind of second father. Murder seemed even less credible. She vacillated between the living room and the kitchen, stopping only to light a cigarette, wishing she could quiet the sick feeling in her stomach.

Other deaths surfaced in her memory: a classmate, their family doctor's son. Both victims of hunting accidents. And FDR—the only president she could remember at that time, another kind of father figure. Three grandparents died before she was old enough to remember; only Dad's mother was still alive—barely.

How would her parents deal with Don's death? Did her father feel guilty? Marty pulled Beethoven's Seventh Symphony from her small record collection, hoping music would ease the tension, loosen the knot in her stomach. Didn't some character in *Point Counter Point* think a Beethoven quartet proved the existence of God?

When first light began to filter through the kitchen window, Marty made a pot of coffee. It was too early to call her parents and Liz would call anyway after she'd made the reservations. *This is one time I need Liz for sure.* She and Liz did not have an easy relationship, though Marty's ambivalence was compounded of love and admiration, as well as envy and competitiveness. She admired Liz's intelligence and the flamboyant style she tried briefly to imitate. But she could never measure up to Liz's bright witty conversations, her innate sense of style.

Unable to stay still, Marty continued to pace, her thoughts focused more on her conversation with Liz than Don's death. *Does she always get family news first because she's the oldest? Or the favored?* As the wild, rhapsodic last movement of the symphony ended, the phone rang again.

"I've got airline reservations for us. And I called the folks."

"I figured *you* would!"

"Well, they need to know when we'll arrive. Marty, for Pete's sake! Can't we bury the hatchet for Mom and Dad's sake? You're the one who said Dad must be devastated."

"I'm really glad you called them. I'm just upset and terribly worried. Dad was closer to Don than to either of his brothers."

"Right. But they'll handle it. Our parents are not fragile."

"Mom is tougher than Dad, though, don't you think? On the inside, not the outside. Maybe because her life was much tougher than his." No need to remind Liz that Mom left home at thirteen to work for room and board, that he graduated from a university and she never finished high school. She would never forget Mom's stories about her family contracting influenza during the First World War and one sister almost dying while Dad's family escaped the epidemic completely.

"He's a politician, Marty. You don't survive that with a thin skin."

"I suppose."

"Do you want to get together this afternoon?"

"No, there's too much to do. We'll have time to talk on the plane. When do we leave?"

"Two thirty. Northwest. We change planes in Minneapolis and arrive about midnight. I'm not sure what they fly into South Dakota, but probably a DC3, one of those two prop planes used in the war. Let's meet at Midway at 1:30 near the ticket counter."

Marty hung up, poured another cup of coffee and lit another cigarette. She picked up yesterday's *Chicago Sun Times* and tried to read, but nothing held her attention. Nothing seemed important.

Suicide or murder? Could anyone have reason to kill such a kind, generous man? But why didn't he talk to her father if he felt desperate? Money was not an issue. He could buy anything he desired, spend the whole summer fishing in Minnesota or Canada if he wanted. He was getting old, like her parents, but he seemed healthy. What he lacked was family, except for distant cousins, since his mother's death. Was it only six years ago Nellie died? Marty could not remember her parents discussing why Don never married; she always assumed his mother was the reason. Nellie, the frail, white-haired lady sitting in her wheel chair, unable to walk after breaking both hips; Don in the background, anticipating her every need, the only offspring, completely devoted. If his father had lived longer, would Don have married? He had never seemed depressed to Marty. But she never really paid attention to him. Yet, he was always there and somehow her family had failed him. *We were the closest he had.*

When the phone rang again, she welcomed the reprieve.

"Hi. Glad you're up. I was afraid I'd wake you."

"Oh Rich, I've had some bad news. Could you come over? Help me get through the day?"

"Sure. What happened?"

"A close friend of the family died. I'll tell you about it when you get here."

"I'm sorry. Be there within the hour. Okay?"

"Thanks. Please hurry."

"I love you."

"Me too."

By the time Richard arrived, Marty had dressed, picked up the apartment, and was looking at pictures of Don in a photo album. When Richard held her, she felt comforted by his broad shoulders, her five feet protected by his much larger frame. But her agitation returned quickly and she pulled away.

"You'd better talk about it," he said, hanging his GI storm coat, a relic of his service in the Occupation Army in Japan, over a chair. "Okay if I sit?"

"Of course. I seem to need to keep moving." She sighed. Momentarily, she felt like giggling. "Please ask me questions. I don't know where to begin."

"Tell me what happened."

"Don Wagner is—was—my father's closest friend. They grew up together, hunted and fished together all their life. Growing up in a city, you probably can't appreciate how important that is—was. I think my parents felt sorry for him because he never married. After Nellie died—that's Don's mother—he ate dinner at our house most Sundays and other times too. Before she died, we vacationed together in Northern Minnesota during the '30s and '40s. We even went during the war, because they allowed Don enough gas to drive there. It was for medical reasons . . . the northern piney woods helped his mother's asthma. Don always drove. He wouldn't let anyone else drive his cars . . . because he'd been a chauffeur in the First World War, according to my Dad. Anyway, Dad and Don fished every day from sunup to sundown. They'd go out in a small motor boat before I was up and come in late with their limit of wall-eyed pike. He treated Liz and me like daughters." Close to tears, Marty slumped on the sofa next to Richard.

"I'm sorry, Marty." Richard reached for her hand.

But Marty pulled away and started to pace. "He did so much for me, but I never felt close to him, not really," she admitted. "He was quiet; he never told me what to do—and I was a kid—and I had parents. My parents were foreground; he was background."

"Marty you were just a kid. You shouldn't feel guilty. How did he die?"

"He shot himself in the head. He left a suicide note to my father. I don't know what he wrote." She paused. "Dad thinks he might have been murdered."

"Why? What would be a motive?"

"Money, I suppose. He's probably the richest man in town. Not Rockefeller rich, but rich for a small South Dakota town."

"Was he robbed?"

"I don't know. It just happened last night. Liz and I are flying to South Dakota tomorrow. Oh, that reminds me. If I need to stay awhile, would you be willing to ask my instructors to give me Incompletes this quarter? Or a Registered in Dr. B's course? I'll never catch up on his assigned readings. And talk to Dr. Martin. He may need to look for a new research assistant."

"You'll be gone that long?"

"I don't know. Don was almost family. His death wasn't natural. What if there's a murder investigation? It really depends on my parents. I doubt Liz can stay because of her job. Poor Dad. My grandmother is bedridden from a stroke she had two months ago and now he has to deal with this."

"Okay. I'll talk to your instructors. I'll even drive you to the airport tomorrow and look after your apartment."

"How can you drive me to the airport?"

"I'll borrow a car from someone at the lab. Don't worry, I'll find a car."

"Thanks. Would you like to move in here while I'm gone? My apartment is bigger and nicer then yours. No offense."

"But it isn't as close to the psych lab. I'd have to walk a lot further to feed the rats and clean cages. Anyway, what's the point? You'd kick me out when you came back."

"You're probably right."

"If we lived together, we could save money. And time."

"It's just not conducive to studying, Rich, and you know I want an advanced degree so I can have an interesting career."

"Marty, I want you to stay in school. I have to study too."

"You hold Bill and Gail's relationship up as close to ideal, but Gail dropped out of graduate school to support Bill through medical school."

"Gail wanted to drop out. If she hadn't, they probably wouldn't have gotten married."

"Yes, that's my point. I don't want to drop out. Gail wanted to get married. I don't . . . yet. Oh, let's not fight."

"You're right. Let's walk over to Bill and Gail's. Maybe go to a movie?"

"Let's walk. I don't think I could sit through a movie."

"Better put on your boots. More snow fell last night and not all the walks are shoveled."

"Okay, okay. I know it's snowy out." Sometimes he irritated her.

They started north on Greenwood; crossed the Midway and turned east outside the university quadrangle; passed Harper Library, Social Sciences, and Foster Hall—the dorm where Marty lived for two years under the watchful eye of Irish maids, where she met and befriended Gail. After Rockefeller Chapel, they took Woodlawn to 61st Street, then 61st toward Bill and Gail's apartment in a three-story, six-unit building that the university rented to graduate students.

Gail sensed Marty's distress immediately and gave her a hug. "What's wrong?"

"You're upset." Bill looked up from a medical text.

"I am." Marty sat on the edge of the sofa after Richard helped her with her coat and told them what had happened.

"I'm so sorry, Marty. I'm glad we got a chance to see you before you leave. Any idea when you'll be back?"

"No. Depends on my parents really."

"How about some coffee? Marty? Rich?" After Marty rejected the coffee she offered, Gail said, "Why don't you come look at the future nursery? The colors are so bright and cheery."

Marty followed her into the only bedroom in the small apartment. "Gail, if the baby has this room, where will you and Bill sleep?"

"In the dining room. Wait 'til you see all the cute things I have." She opened two dresser drawers filled with tiny articles of clothing and bedding.

Marty tried to be enthusiastic, but Gail's nesting behavior only made her feel worse. "Gail, I've got to leave, I've got to keep moving. Sorry, Bill. I'm gonna drag Rich away. I don't know how soon I'll see you again, but we can communicate through Rich. Gail, take care of yourself."

Back on 61st Street, they walked toward 60th and the Midway. Richard rambled on about the flicker fusion work he was doing for one of his professors and ideas he was generating for a doctoral dissertation.

Marty half-listened until they came to the statue of Mazaryk on the Midway. "Someday I'm going to find out why there is a monument here to the first president of Czechoslovakia. Do you know?"

"No. But International House is nearby."

Eventually, they arrived at Lake Michigan—a frozen ice field, forbidding in February, yet providing the broad vista, the occasional safety valve for Marty's periodic, claustrophobic reaction when city structures closed in on her. From the point off 55th Street they could see the great expanse of the Chicago skyline which extended north toward and beyond the Gold Coast. Fierce, penetrating wind whipped around them. When Marty began to shiver, Richard put his arm around her shoulder, enveloping her in his heavy parka.

"I like this place better in the summer," Marty said. "Let's go."

They retreated to 53rd Street and entered a small restaurant. Marty ordered coffee and a toasted muffin that she pushed aside after one bite. She watched Richard down a cheeseburger, a piece of apple pie, and finally her muffin.

"You really should try to eat," he said, "to keep up your strength."

"You sound like my mother. I doubt missing a meal or two really matters. It feels strange though. I've never not had an appetite before."

By the time they entered the campus through Hull Gate and walked past Botany Pond, the sky had darkened from slate to charcoal gray. Approaching the central quadrangle, they stopped to listen to the carillon in Rockefeller Chapel.

Marty sighed. "It's perfect. The music, the neo-gothic architecture, the gargoyles, the walkways, the light posts. There's no other place like it."

"Should we sit?" Richard brushed snow off the C Bench.

"Do you think people can imprint on their *alma mater*? Like some birds do to a moving object at a critical age?" Marty cuddled next to him.

"No." He laughed. "Maybe their football teams. But love and loyalty are not imprinting. Do you feel that intensely about Chicago?"

"Yes, I'm imprinted!" She laughed too. "Oh, Rich, I should be at the lab helping you with the rats."

"That's okay. I'll go first thing in the morning."

Approaching her apartment, Marty hesitated. "Rich, thanks for helping me through the day. You've been great, but I need to be alone now. For one thing—to pack. I'm sorry. Okay?"

"What can I say? I'd like to think my presence is comforting."

If Marty heard any hurt or annoyance in his voice, she chose to ignore it. "Look, I'll see you tomorrow. I really appreciate your driving me."

When Richard arrived at Marty's the next day he found her two suitcases near the door and Marty ready to leave.

"Feeling any better?" He picked up her suitcases.

"My stomach is better, but I'm tired. I know I slept, but it seems like I had bad dreams all night."

Driving down 55th Street, he tried to engage her in conversation. "Interested in hearing about Spence's new research project?"

"I'm so tired, I don't think it would register. My only interest is getting to South Dakota. I won't even complain about the row upon row of identical, ugly bungalows on this street."

"Well, that's a switch. Any more instructions for me about your place?"

"Just don't forget to water the plants and take the mail in."

When they arrived at Midway Airport, Richard retrieved Marty's bags from the car and they headed for the terminal. Seeing Liz as they entered, he turned to Marty, "You will write to me—often, I hope."

"Of course, whenever I can. You'll write too, right?" Marty guessed he wanted to reach out, to comfort her, break through her formal farewell, but her demeanor and Liz's approach held him back. Impulsively, she grabbed his hands to let him know she understood.

Liz motioned them to follow her to the Northwest ticket area. Marty, certain Liz eyed her bulging suitcases with disapproval, said defensively, "I'm the one who'll stay, if necessary."

"I know. It's impossible for me to stay even a week. You can't imagine how tough work is right now."

Putting Liz on the defensive gave Marty a flicker of satisfaction. "I hope I don't lose course credit by not being in school." Immediately, she regretted her pettiness and was glad Liz ignored it.

Richard stood in line with them until Marty's bag got checked through. "I should go. Have a good flight, you two. I'm sorry about what you have to face in South Dakota." He gave Marty a quick peck on the cheek and left.

"We have half an hour or so," Liz said, looking at her watch. "Let's get coffee."

Marty had never flown commercially before, only on tiny seaplanes from one lake to another in the north woods of Minnesota and Manitoba with her parents and Don. Already anxious, she jammed her hands, cold and clammy, into her pockets. As an undergraduate, she usually took the Dakota 400 to and from Chicago, but one Christmas vacation she traveled on a milk train that took forever to cross the flat, snow-covered, infinite prairie. On that trip she discovered the center of her world was, in reality, a remote town in the vast heartland of the country hundreds of miles from the center of anything. It would always be home, even though it felt different after that. She still liked trains, felt certain they were safer and more comfortable than planes. She liked walking to the club car or diner or the smoking area when she got tired of reading or looking out at the endless, horizontal landscape of southern Minnesota and east central South Dakota.

Once in the air Marty relaxed somewhat, although she gave up trying to nap when she began to have scary dreams. Eyes open, she marveled at Liz, engrossed in a paperback she snitched from Marty's bag. "Liz, you finding Stud's life on the South Side interesting?"

"Sort of. I like reading about Chicago neighborhoods and the university during the post First World War era. Interesting contrasts . . . the South Side then and now, growing up in a big city neighborhood compared to our small town. You know, Chicago freed us from a lot of small town constraints."

"I'll say. And magnified our intellectual and cultural pretensions. Anyway, I could be a perennial student, put off facing the 'real world' indefinitely."

"Well right now we need to face the real world." Liz put her book down and lit a cigarette. "One of us should check with Don's doctor. Didn't Mom worry about his health a while back?"

"Yes, but nothing came of it. It's hard to believe Don committed suicide without a good reason, though—like a serious illness."

"For whatever reason, he must have felt desperate. Why didn't he talk to Dad?" Liz shook her head.

"I wonder if that would have done any good? He had lots of friends besides Dad and long-time employees. I don't think anything makes up for family—someone to come home to every evening, every weekend. Since Nellie's death, he's lived alone in that big, old house."

"Do you remember Mom saying that Don asked her to stay at his house on the night of Nellie's funeral? Dad left for Pierre right after the burial. Of course Mom said no. I'm sure she worried about what the neighbors might think!"

"I remember being surprised. Not that Mom didn't stay as much as his asking. Maybe he was less conventional than he seemed."

"Or more lonely. When I saw him at Christmas, he talked a lot about Grandma. Her illness must have reminded him of his own mother"

"And his own vulnerability. What would happen if he had a stroke? Who would care for him? You know, we both talk as if we've accepted his death as a suicide. Oh, it's so sad, Liz. I hope Dad isn't blaming himself."

"Before you get too weepy, tighten your seat belt. I think we're about to descend."

Snow was falling in Minneapolis. "Can you believe this town produced F. Scott Fitzgerald?" Marty exclaimed, brushing snow off her coat once inside the airport.

"It was St. Paul," Liz corrected. "Anyway, what's your point?"

"He just seems southern. Zelda's influence, I guess."

"Don't you remember *Winter Dreams* and the *Ice Palace*? Even Gatsby was from Northern Minnesota, I think. Duluth?"

"Okay, okay."

Later, as they sipped after-dinner coffee and waited to board the DC3 and begin the last lap of the trip, Liz said, "Do you suppose anyone will think Dad killed Don?"

"How could they?" Marty stopped short, a visual image of her father punching a reporter, an incident she had only read about in the newspaper. "God, I hope not." *But why not, since he may be the one who benefits the most financially?*

Chapter Three

Back on Campus

Driving back to campus on 55th street, Richard smiled as he passed the blocks of bungalows, remembering Marty's sarcastic comments about the inevitable lamp in the inevitable picture window—symbols of the conventionality she loved to hate. Not exactly Frank Lloyd Wright or Sullivan creations. He hadn't told her his parents lived in a comparable blue-collar neighborhood.

Marty kept him off balance ever since they took a graduate course in genetics. His intense need for her was a new experience—a neurosis. At the very least, an obsession. He wished it were mutual. But being with him was not as necessary for her as being with her was for him. Still, he knew she cared.

As he approached Ellis Avenue, Richard shifted gears physically and mentally. He needed to return the car and clean the cages he missed in the morning. He might even find someone to have dinner with, to kill time, to keep from being lonely. He missed Marty already. He decided to look for her instructors on Wednesday, one of her regular class days. Marty's request for either an Incomplete or Registered would undoubtedly be granted, but he'd check first to make sure she didn't lose course credit.

Richard parked behind the university bookstore and headed toward the Psychology Department's animal lab, a slowly disintegrating pre-fab, already abandoned, according to a circulating joke, by the wild rats. Blocks of these temporary post-war structures provided housing for married veterans who descended on campus after WWII in droves. A cheap possibility for him and Marty, if she'd agree to marry.

Opening the door to the lab, Richard braced himself for the several and separate odors co-mingled forever in the masonite walls. The chorus that greeted him, the cacophony of animal sounds and the rattle and clang of cages, was more welcoming, if not exactly *The Ode To Joy*.

"Hey, Rich. I thought you and Marty were spending afternoons in the library this week." Spence, a fellow student, entered the hallway carrying an empty cage.

"It's a long story. She went home, a death in the family. Is Pete around?"

"Somewhere. Try the storeroom."

"Want to go to Jimmy's later for a beer and hamburger? After I find Pete and take care of the rats."

"Sure, I'll be through running cats in an hour or two. I'd like to go out. Anything to escape George for awhile."

"George? What's the problem?"

"I'll tell you about it later."

Richard found Pete reorganizing equipment in the storeroom. "Thanks for the car, Pete."

"You're welcome. How's Marty?"

"Quiet. Not herself. Want to join Spence and me at Jimmy's later?"

"I can't tonight. I've got too much to do."

"Don't forget you agreed to be a subject tomorrow."

"I'll be there. The room adjacent to Hathaway's office?"

"Right."

They pushed their way through the crowd to a table in the back of Jimmy's. "It never occurred to me this place would be so busy on Monday. Marty and I usually come here on Friday or Saturday. It's always mobbed then."

"Most students don't care what night it is when it comes to drinking beer. Speaking of Marty, what's the story?"

"A close friend of the family died. Probably a suicide. I'll try to get up to the bar and order us a pitcher of beer. Want a hamburger?"

"Two."

Richard returned with a pitcher and two glasses. "They'll deliver the burgers when they're ready."

"What were you saying about Marty?" Spence poured the beer.

"She didn't have much information. She's mostly worried about her parents. Not sure how they'll take it, so she doesn't know when she'll return. I already miss her."

Spence laughed. "I wish George would visit his parents. He's a pain to live with. Ever since his course on nondirective therapy with Carl Rogers."

"Marty took that course, but she's more interested in research than counseling. Does George reflect à la Rogers?" Richard made quotation marks around *reflects* with his fingers. "Oh good. Here are our hamburgers."

"If I complain about the apartment, George says, 'Oh, you think the place is a mess.' In fact, the place is littered with his papers and dirty clothes. But getting back to the important thing—research—how do you like working for Hathaway?" Spence poured more beer into their glasses.

"I like him; he's basically a behaviorist, but he's not close-minded. Want to be a subject in a study I'm doing for him on flicker fusion?"

"What do I have to do?"

"Sit in a dark room and tell me when the still pictures fuse into a moving picture, when the flicker disappears."

"Is Hathaway working for the movie industry?"

"Not that I'm aware of." Richard laughed.

"I'll be a subject if you'll help me design and build equipment for one of my projects." Spence described what he had in mind.

"Okay. I like honing my inventive skills. We can figure out a good time tomorrow at the lab. Should we call it a night?"

"Sure. The beer is gone and I'm ready to hit the hay." They left cash at the bar and parted at the door, going in opposite directions on 55th Street.

Before heading to his place, Richard detoured to Marty's apartment. Everything seemed in order: windows locked, kitchen cleaned up. He sat on her couch and picked up the photo album from the makeshift shipping crate/coffee table. Turning the pages, he saw snapshots of Marty and Liz in high school; their parents, Ellen and CB—the C stood for Charles but Marty never told him what the middle initial stood for; and Boots, the family dog. When he came to a picture of CB and another man holding a big string of fish, he assumed the second man was Don. Tall, thin, bald, he had a long narrow face. Did he look bemused or somber? Preoccupied, not grim. *This man took his own life?* Richard couldn't imagine it since life seemed infinitely interesting. *But I don't know how I'll feel in forty years; who knows what life feels like at 60?*

He found another photo of Don in a group shot with a young Marty, her parents, and a white-haired lady in a wheelchair—Don's mother, he guessed. Liz probably took the picture on vacation in Minnesota, judging by the pine trees and log cabin in the background. Though her head was downcast, Marty's long, dark hair did not conceal her high cheekbones nor the smirk conveyed by her one-sided smile and the thin, determined lips. But his favorite photograph showed Marty in shorts—her twisted mouth reflecting a struggle—holding up a fish almost as tall as she was. In several photographs he saw Marty's strong resemblance to her mother, Ellen, an attractive woman whose dark hair contributed to her youthful appearance. He remembered Marty's comment about her mother being a "typical housewife basically subservient to her husband."

Charles B. Black looked stern, Prussian, with his full head of short, steel-gray hair. Richard knew he could be abrupt, gruff and off-putting. He met the Blacks the previous summer when they came to Chicago for the National Republican Convention that nominated Eisenhower. Impressed that Marty's father was a delegate, Richard approached political discussions with caution, since he was a New Deal Democrat, far left of CB. Still, CB proved more reasonable than he expected a Taft Republican to be.

Richard scanned several snapshots of young girls he guessed were high school friends. In one photo he recognized Carl, an old college boyfriend of Marty's, who recently married another classmate. Richard, still jealous of the time Marty spent with Carl, occasionally wanted reassurance she had no lingering feelings.

Before he closed the album, Richard studied the picture of another young man. This must be Wally, the high school boyfriend and football star, flanked in the photo by two cheerleaders. Marty's reference to him as her first love had a nostalgic quality, but when Richard pressed her for details, she dismissed him as a rogue or a rake or some other undesirable type. Richard wasn't surprised: he believed men of questionable character attracted women.

He liked the idea of being close to Marty's things, and he briefly reconsidered moving in here. Maybe the move *would* be permanent. Wishful thinking, not realistic. And the effort required to move would hardly be worth it if she returned soon. He decided to wait and see what developed. As he was leaving, he noticed her slippers next to the small telephone table. He picked one up, slipped his hand into it. She once told him her feet were her best feature—long, narrow, with unblemished toes—and she should meet a man with a foot fetish.

As he was locking up, the student living in the other basement apartment, opened his door. "Marty said you'd be checking her apartment. Come on over and have a beer."

"Thanks, Ed. Not tonight. I'm beat."

Later in his own apartment, Richard resisted an urge to call. Marty might not be home yet. If she were, it would be an emotional time with her family. Anyway, Marty would consider a phone call this soon as foolish. She'd be annoyed. She would respect restraint more than neurotic neediness. He turned on the radio for news. No plane crashes. Finally, his need to be with her, to talk to her, to share the thoughts he'd directed toward her all day got the better of him. He sat down to write.

Dear Marty,

As soon as I left the airport I began to have imaginary conversations with you. And that's been happening ever since—even when I'm talking with someone else. I love you.

He stopped. Best to report the events of the day. He wrote about the lab, eating with Spence and their conversation about nondirective therapy, his checking her apartment and looking at her photo album. He ended:

I hope you and your parents are doing okay.

I Love You, Bushel and a Peck
Rich

He almost looked forward to finding Marty's instructors and the professor who hired her to analyze psychological test data. It gave him an excuse to talk about her. But he should get on with things. He had plenty of work to keep him busy and friends to socialize with. He should focus on those things and not fret about her.

Chapter Four

The Homecoming

Marty and Liz stood transfixed by the view from inside the Minneapolis airport. "Should we worry about this weather?" Marty asked, staring at the thickening blanket of snow.

"No, worrywort. They won't fly if it's too bad. Looks like we could spend the night here, though. Let's go have a drink."

Following Liz's lead, Marty ordered a scotch and soda, hoping it would help her relax. She admired Liz's calm, her seeming detachment, even as they talked about what they might be facing at home. She learned that Liz had no intentions of staying more than a few days, probably leaving right after the funeral. Marty accepted it. Liz needed to get on with her career; Marty was a student with less at stake.

"Liz, what if Dad is accused? I'm not sure I can handle it."

"Be there for them. Marty, don't forget our family is respected; Dad is above suspicion."

"I hope you're right, but he has alienated people by being outspoken. He's very opinionated. He's guilty of name calling at the city commission meetings, and he actually socked a reporter once when he was in Pierre."

"Let's go. They just called our flight. It must have stopped snowing."

Marty followed Liz to the gate.

Twice the DC3 taxied to the end of the runway, then returned because one prop was missing badly. Marty, who could see the prop from her seat, was grateful when the flight was canceled. After a call home, they boarded a bus at 2:00 a.m. to be taken to a nearby hotel, courtesy of the airline. Without luggage, Marty fell asleep in her slip, too exhausted to miss her toothbrush or care about the shabby room, which Liz likened to a hangout in a 1940s gangster movie. Four hours later, awakened by a call informing them of a rescheduled flight, they gulped down orange juice and coffee before boarding another bus.

As they took off once again, Marty braced herself for the noisy engines, sighing with relief when the props ran smoothly. She settled into her seat next to Liz and closed her eyes to shut out the dense fog pressing against her window. Peeking a few moments later, she brightened in the sun's glow, bedazzled by the cobalt sky and the billowy clouds, heaps of whipped cream beneath them. Fear surfaced when the plane circled repeatedly, hawk-like, above gray, ominous clouds. When they finally nosed down, Marty took a deep breath, as if she were preparing to dive.

Suddenly she saw the ground, the hangars, and a small group of people near the terminal. Even before they landed, she could make out her parents, tiny figures near the fence. Thankful to be here at last, she got off the plane and crossed the tarmac eager to get to the gate.

Inside the fence Marty skirted the group and rushed up to her parents, arms outstretched. "Mom! Dad!"

"Thank goodness you're here." Ellen hugged her, then reached for Liz.

"Thanks for coming girls. We need you." CB kissed Marty on top of her head as he extended an arm to Liz. "It's cold out here. Let's go in and get your luggage."

Marty and Liz retrieved their bags and followed their parents to the car. Ellen, dark circles under her eyes, sat quietly next to CB and occasionally glanced back at her daughters. CB hardly stopped talking as he drove toward town, but Liz finally found the moment to ask, "Dad, when is the funeral?"

"Tomorrow at 2:00. We'll be the mourners with Don's two cousins."

Marty held her breath, wondering what Liz would say. But Liz only glanced at her, then looked out the window. *She'll wait to tell them she can't stay long.*

As they drove into town, Marty watched for changes along the highway. She loved the flat, open country—almost treeless, except for shelter-belts, those guardians of the soil—an horizon approaching 360 degrees. She felt close to the sky and God, when she believed in Him. A fresh, white mantle of snow disguised the shabbiness of an occasional modest structure on this stretch of road. After crossing the Chicago Northwestern railroad tracks, they headed toward the main intersection in town and beyond to Fifth Street where they turned. On that corner they passed the Presbyterian Church—large, austere, without a steeple—where they would congregate for Don's funeral.

The Black's house was four blocks east at the corner of Idaho and Fifth. This plain white duplex with green trim was originally a single family Queen Anne Victorian like so many other houses in this town settled in the early 1880s. Her father lived here as a child. Renovations in the '20s removed the elaborate trim and the wrap-around porch and converted three rooms on the south side of the house into an apartment for CB's widowed mother. Don grew up in a similar house next door until he and Nellie, also widowed, built a modern brick house on the other side of town about the time of Marty's birth. The Black's new neighbors included Mary Alice—two years older than Marty—who married and had a baby before Marty graduated high school.

Inside, the upright Gilbranson and the bench filled with five or six volumes of *Schirmer's Library of Musical Classics* and sheet music stood in one corner of the dining room opposite a large, claw-footed China cabinet. Marty suppressed an impulse to play the piano before lunch when CB said he was hungry. But after Ellen, Liz, and Marty rushed to get soup and crackers, cheese and fruit on the table, no one ate much.

Still tense and garrulous, CB told his story again. "Don stayed home from work on Saturday—probably the first time in his 64 years. About midmorning he called to ask Bob Meyer to come to the house to do a favor."

"Who's Bob Meyer?" Liz asked.

"Don's right hand at the store. You remember him. He's worked there over 20 years."

"He's the short, thin one. Going bald," Marty added.

CB repeated Meyer's story about going to the bank to cash a check for $9,500, returning with the money, and going back to the store without knowing why Don wanted the money.

"Dad, did you go into the store or call Don that day?" Liz asked.

"I called him about 1:30 when I discovered he wasn't in the store and kidded him about playing hooky. He sounded in good spirits. He said he had a business deal he was attending to. I asked if he was still planning to have dinner with us on Sunday and he said he was. According to Meyer, Don called his store around 5:30 or 6:00 to say he'd meet Erickson at 7:00 that evening."

"Who's Erickson?" Marty asked.

"A salesman Don orders hardware from." He told them about Erickson's call and his effort to locate Don.

Ellen interrupted, "I began to wonder if he had fallen, had a stroke, or something."

CB continued his description of the two trips to the house and hearing about the money from Bob Meyer. His speech broke when he described finding Don on his bed soaked in blood.

"Oh how horrible," Liz covered her mouth. Marty put her hand on her father's arm.

CB sighed deeply. "We called the coroner and the police. The coroner found the suicide note." He stopped, unable to go on. Ellen got up and left the room. Both Marty and Liz sat quietly, stunned.

Liz broke the silence. "Dad, what did the note say?"

"The coroner has it. Something about being lonely. There was more but I only had a second to look at it."

"Go on, Dad," Marty said.

"He died between 6:30 and 7:00P.M. There were two bullet wounds—the first bullet entered at the back of the neck, hit an artery but missed any vital centers. The second entered the temple and pierced the brain. The coroner said the second bullet was considerably later than the first and Don bled to death."

Marty got up from the table to escape her father's pain and to look for her mother. Ellen, staring out the large dining room window, turned when Marty entered the room.

"Oh Marty, it's so sad! Don wrote in the note that he was lonely and he wanted to talk to your father, but he couldn't." Ellen began to get teary. "He also said his friends would be better off with him dead than alive. Then 'Goodbye, Don.'"

"I'm so sorry, Mom." Marty wrapped her arms around her mother and held her tight.

Before CB left to meet with investigators opening Don's safely deposit box, he told Liz and Marty he suspected foul play—possibly murder—because the money withdrawn from Don's bank account was unaccounted for. He hoped papers in the box would provide some clues.

Liz and Marty finally convinced Ellen to try to nap. They recognized her exhaustion, but her frequent teariness surprised

Marty. No one in this family cried. She volunteered to stay home and answer the phone or doorbell, so Ellen could rest, while Liz went searching for medical evidence at the clinic where Don's doctor practiced.

Knowing she would keep her mother awake if she played the piano, Marty scanned the bookshelves for something to read. But interrupted by phone calls and preoccupied with her Dad's earlier narrative, she could not choose. Most callers offered sympathy; a few sought information about the death. She was unprepared for the unidentified caller who asked, "What did you do with the money?" and hung up. Shaken, her first impulse was to hide rather than answer the doorbell when it rang a few minutes later. She dreaded the thought of a visitor. But when the doorbell rang a second time, she opened the door and saw an old friend.

Jessie, a neighbor and political colleague of CB's, grew up and went to school with CB and Don. Inspired by her suffragette mother, she rose to political prominence early in life. She was a candidate for governor in 1930 and served briefly in the U.S. Senate in the late '30s, appointed by the governor to fill out a term. Tall, stately, regal, Jessie reminded Marty of Eleanor Roosevelt—a comparison, Marty realized, that might offend her, a dedicated Republican.

Marty wondered why Jessie never married. Was it her fierce independence? Or, because, like Don, she took on the care of an aging, widowed parent? Alone, she survived primarily by renting the upstairs of her large Victorian house to two women. She came, now, to say "Hello," to catch up on and commiserate with Liz and Marty—young women she watched grow up—and to tell Ellen about the church women's plans for dinner the next day.

Before they got to the kitchen for coffee and the muffins Jessie baked, she asked, "How's your father?"

Marty shook her head. "Taking it pretty hard as you can imagine. He's not convinced Don committed suicide."

"I have doubts too. Don wouldn't do that to your father. He knew your father was already going through a tough time with your grandmother."

Ellen joined them, and a few minutes later Liz returned.

"The records show that Don visited the clinic two years ago for a routine physical. No serious diagnoses," she announced.

CB also had little to report when he got home. "The safety deposit box was filled with documents, but nothing that throws light on the missing money. And nothing in the will."

Restless, he paced from the living room to the kitchen and back. "Liz, Marty. Will you girls come with me to visit your grandmother?"

Marty, ambivalent about seeing this beloved childhood figure—Grandma Martha, for whom she was named—knew she had no choice. "Sure, Dad. Liz, grab our coats, and I'll go tell Mom where we're going." She headed for the kitchen.

"Marty, it will be hard." Ellen spoke in a low voice so CB couldn't hear. "She won't know you. Some days your dad thinks she's getting better, but I'm not sure he really believes it."

Despite her mother's warning, Marty was unprepared to see her grandmother in a crib-like bed, mumbling nonsense, picking at the quilt with gnarled fingers. Marty gently took one of her grandmother's hands and kissed her wrinkled forehead. "Hi, Grandma. It's Marty. I'm home from Chicago. It's good to see you." What else could she say? Did it matter? When Liz moved closer, Marty stepped aside, staring at the blue-veined hand, skin as thin as filo dough, remembering how it felt as a child to have this hand holding hers. Later, as an adolescent interested in piano, she wished she had inherited Ellen's long, tapering fingers instead of Martha's short, knobby ones. She wondered if her grandmother knew she was there. Her eyes followed sometimes, but what did they see? What memories were intact? Occasionally, a word emerged from the sounds she made without a meaningful context.

When they returned to the car, CB said, "Mother's doing better here in Mrs. Robert's home. Mrs. Roberts only has five women to care for so they get the attention they need. In the hospital they kept giving her shots to keep her quiet."

"Why?" Liz asked.

"She was singing hymns at all hours—the hymns she sang in the church choir when she was young."

At dinner CB told them about Don's will. "He left money to the college and the church, and he willed his land near the river to the town for a park. He left all his employees money and he left me one farm—maybe two. I didn't have time to read the entire will or the codicils, so I don't know all the details."

"Dad, any idea if he missed someone, someone who might be the intended for the missing money? Like Jessie, maybe," Marty suggested.

"Don knew she struggled financially, but she'd let us know."

"You don't think she'd worry about a scandal?" Liz questioned.

"Maybe she hasn't received the money yet." Marty added.

"It seems unlikely that anyone received the money on Saturday. No one saw Don leave his house, and there were no tire tracks in the snow from his car or truck. No sign he went to the post office or anywhere. And the post office hasn't found anything. That's why I think someone was in the house with Don and got the money."

Marty shook her head. "I think the money will show up. Maybe in the house with a note."

Later that night Marty wrote her first letter to Richard. After describing the scary flight, the events that preceded Don's death, what she knew about his will and the suicide note, she continued:

> Rich, Dad is haunted by the death scene which he describes over and over again. At first it nauseated me, but he seemed less nervous tonight. Maybe the repetition is good. He thinks someone

was blackmailing Don. Another possibility: Don wanted to give money to someone he missed in his will. We're hoping it is in the house with a note of explanation, since there is no evidence Don left the house to mail or deliver it. Investigation proceeds on all these and other angles.

Rich, honey, it's 2:30 a.m. and I've got to get to sleep. The funeral is tomorrow—another grueling ordeal. I'll write more tomorrow and I'll send newspaper clippings if I can find some. Mother sent our copies to Don's relatives.

Please write a lot. I look forward to your letters. I really miss you. (And I'm pretty sure now I'm stuck here for awhile.)

I love you,
Marty

PS: Don't forget to talk to my professors.

Chapter Five

The Funeral

Awakened the next morning by her sister's voice, Marty almost leaped out of bed to get ready for school. The room, the flowered wallpaper, Liz—for a moment Marty had never left home.

"I just saw the church women drive up. You'd better hurry. They're here to feed the mourners, you know—that's us and the cousins, too, of course. We're being treated like family." Liz was putting on makeup, sitting at the simple, Art Deco dressing table with its flowered skirt, glass tabletop, matching lamps, and round mirror that Ellen ordered from Sears and assembled when Liz was in junior high school. Her long, dark hair was short now; the skirt, sweater, and saddle shoes, replaced by a suit, scarf, and heels—always stylish. *She has flair. No wonder I've envied her.*

"Go ahead. I'll be ready in a minute." Marty watched Liz leave the room. She wanted to re-experience this room alone, the room she slept in throughout her childhood, the room she cleaned every Saturday morning during her high school years while she listened to *Grand Central Station* on the radio. Although she no longer remembered the other programs, she could still hear Billy Burke's high-pitched, unique voice. When she finished cleaning—usually by noon—she was free to see friends. Friends! How quickly they scattered to Minneapolis, Des Moine, Salt Lake City, San Diego and Berkeley. Most of her peers went west after high school—even Wally, her first and only high school boyfriend. She was trying to reconstruct the last argument she had with him, a silly fight about California, when Liz appeared in the doorway.

"C'mon, Marty. What's taking you so long?"

"Liz, did all your friends go west after high school? Is it a Midwestern thing?"

"No. Joan went east and so did you and I. If you grow up here, you have to go somewhere. Not much reason to stay here unless you inherit a family farm or business or marry into one. Historically, though, movement in this country has been west, toward the frontier. During the '30s the dust storms and the Depression drove hundreds of families to California looking for work—like the Joads."

"Thanks for the history lesson. I was just wondering about your friends."

"Did all your friends go west?"

"Most of them. Cathy and Mary Alice are here. I'll look them up next week."

"Marty, we really have to get downstairs. I've got good news. No cousins for dinner. We're meeting them at the church."

"Liz, I don't know what to say to the church ladies. I have nothing in common with these Bible belt types, and I'm afraid I might upset Mom."

"Marty, there are only three women downstairs and you know at least two of them: Betty Young and Mrs. Pierce—I don't remember her first name. There's also a Helen McNeill who I don't think was here in the old days. Didn't you go to school with one of the Pierce boys?"

"Yes. Howard."

"Ask about him. Marty, even you can make small talk for ten minutes."

Before Marty sat down with her family, she greeted the other church women and then addressed Mrs. Pierce. "Your son, Howard, and I were in the same Sunday school class for years, but I haven't seen him since high school. How is he?"

"Fine, thank you. He got married last month to a wonderful girl from DeSmet."

"Congratulations. That's great."

"Are you married, Marty?"

"No. I'm still in school."

"Well, you have plenty of time, dear." She patted Marty's arm. "Do Howard and his wife live in town?"

"No. Howard is still in the service and he may stay in. But he's back from Korea. Thank the Lord! They may be moving around the country for quite awhile. Oh, I'd better go help Betty with the hot dishes before she starts wondering about me. I'll tell him you asked for him."

"Thanks. Give them both my best."

Marty sat down next to her father at a table covered with hot dishes, salads, and breads—generous contributions of the ladies auxiliary. Still lacking an appetite, she played with her food, occasionally taking a bite, not wanting to appear unappreciative of these thoughtful women. *Mom certainly taught us manners, if nothing else.*

Long before the 2:00 funeral, the Blacks arrived at the church to meet Don's cousins, both from out of state. Marty recognized the younger one, Gordon, because he visited Don once or twice when Marty was in high school.

"Hi Gordon. I'm sorry we meet again under such sad circumstances."

"Yes. You know, I only saw Don about four times, but he seemed nice."

"He was. Did you ever get a chance to go fishing with him?"

"No. I knew he loved it. Didn't he do most of his fishing in Minnesota?"

"Yeah. I mentioned it because my favorite memory of him was his catching a 25 pound northern pike while Dad and I were trolling with him in Lake Kabetogama."

"That must have been exciting. Even little pike can put up a good fight."

"Don was so skilled, so calm, Dad and I had no idea he had such a large fish until it was right up next to the boat. That's when Dad grabbed the net and helped bring him in. I have proof it's not just a 'fish story.' Don took a snapshot of me holding the fish. It's half as long as I am tall."

"I've never caught anything near that size. Oh. It looks like it's time to join the others."

They took their seats in the back of the church in a small room that opened onto a large, unadorned space with a plain, wooden pulpit up front; pews for the congregation; an organ and choir loft to the right. Marty preferred the Catholic Church down the street with its elaborate altar and statues. But this stark, cavernous structure held many memories from childhood: Sunday school, Christmas programs, junior choir, youth fellowship meetings. She focused on the choir to keep from thinking about the funeral, looking for singers she knew when she sang in the junior choir. She identified Raymond Bell and Margaret Cranston before Dr. Castle appeared in his black robe and began the service.

"We've come together today to say goodbye, to bury a good, honorable man who many of us have known most of our lives." Marty had always admired this "philosopher king" type and his non-preachy sermons, but as he quoted scripture and continued the eulogy, she struggled to keep her composure, looking again toward the choir. But phrases registered: " . . . sacrificed for his mother . . . gave to many . . . let the farmers buy on credit, knowing he'd never get paid . . . could not ask for help . . . felt hopeless."

As he talked about Don's character, including "his tragic flaw—his inability to share his loneliness," she discerned a message to her father and other friends of Don's. If she read something into the message, she hoped her father did also.

When the service ended, the organist began the recessional and the mourners moved slowly, quietly toward the open casket. Liz whispered to Marty, "I'm not going to view the body. It's a pagan ritual."

"Pagan or not, I don't want to either. I prefer to remember Don sitting at our dining room table."

Filing out of the church, the family followed Mr. Webster, the funeral director, to the lead car directly behind the hearse that carried the coffin. Marty purposefully sat on the jump seat to avoid looking at the back of the driver, a young man who dated her once in high school and later told a mutual friend that she didn't know how to kiss. As she watched the line of cars through the rear window, the phrase, "I Love a Parade," resounded in her head all the way to the edge of town and the cemetery road, ending where the parade ended, near a large monument with the name, WAGNER, chiseled into its center. The gaping hole beneath, adjacent to Nellie's modest stone, would be Don's final resting place.

They stood briefly near the casket over the open grave, each lost in private thoughts, while Dr. Castle said a few words. When Marty heard, "ashes to ashes . . ." she could no longer hold back her tears—tears for her father as much as anyone. Somberly they returned to the cars and the church basement for refreshments.

Sipping coffee, nibbling on a sugar cookie, Marty stood looking around this diminished space which evoked memories of church potlucks, Girl Scout meetings, and preparations for the Christmas programs. Only adults posed as Mary and Joseph, but even she got to wear makeup as an angel or shepherd.

She was looking at the small group around Liz when Dr. Castle approached her. "It was so good of you and Liz to come home now. Your parents really need you."

"Oh, Dr. Castle. I know. We wanted to be here." *Does he feel sorry for me because Liz is getting all the attention? Liz's public persona is more extroverted than mine. She's always been more outgoing, more entertaining.* "Both of us are so sad about Don's death."

In the evening the Blacks dined at Laura and Jim Schmidt's house. Jim had worked in Don's hardware store longer than any employee except Bob Meyer. Meyer and his wife, two younger employees of Don's, and Don's cousins were also invited. Conversation centered mostly on the implications of the missing money, on the possibility of someone being in the house with Don, demanding payment. For what? Don's life—without wine, women, or song that anyone knew about—did not seem to have any skeletons.

Marty and Liz listened quietly as the events of that day were reviewed again in detail. On the way home, Marty said to Liz, "I feel sorry for Meyer. He was too trusting. I got the impression he's feeling pretty stupid for not asking questions."

From the front seat CB added, "I think the reason Don asked Meyer and not Jim Schmidt is because Schmidt is a lot sharper."

Hal Mason, another friend of CB's, dropped by later that evening. A former state patrolman, he still looked the part in his ten gallon hat and boots. He criticized the coroner and police chief. "Damn idiots. They assumed suicide, didn't wear gloves or check for fingerprints, and let the neighbors come in and wander through the house. Didn't check powder burns either."

"The authorities botched it," Liz summarized.

"You betcha, we'd have a lot more information if they'd been careful."

"Hal, why did Don use a .22 pistol?" CB asked. "Why not use his most powerful weapon, get the job done the first time?"

"A pistol is easier to handle than a rifle."

Marty had questions she decided not to ask, wanting to spare her father. Why did Don bathe and put on his suit jacket and first shoot himself behind the ear? Was that vanity? Marty did not want to think about—and no one ever mentioned—what went on in Don's head between the two shots.

Getting ready for bed, Marty and Liz continued to speculate. "What do you honestly think happened to the money?" Liz asked.

"I don't know. I was hoping Jessie got it but she would have said something. Unless . . . she hasn't received it yet. Could it be in Don's house? You know, Nellie had private nurses for a few years. Maybe Don felt indebted to one of them. The last nurse lived in his house. Maybe she got through his reserve."

"Isn't Dad convinced Don never got involved with a woman? He knew Don better than anyone." Liz dabbed face cream on her cheeks.

"I'm beginning to wonder if any of us knew Don, including Dad. But you'd think a woman would have come forward by now."

"Maybe not. This is a small town, reason enough to be circumspect, but also likely someone would know about an affair. Well, I can't think any more. I'm going to sleep." Liz turned off her light.

"Mind if I write a letter?" Marty asked.

"To Rich? No. Nothing could keep me awake."

Marty wished she could snuggle in Rich's arms, talk to him about all this. She thought about phoning but she knew her parents thought only dire circumstances warranted long distance phone calls. So she picked up her pen.

Dear Rich,

Please write a lot. About anything. I miss you. I feel like I've been here a month already. Today was so busy, I still haven't unpacked. At least the funeral is over. Rev. Castle gave a wonderful eulogy, full of anecdotes from Don's life. None of us looked at the body, although Dad saw it earlier today. The undertaker encouraged it, I think, believing it might help Dad to see Don in a better state than the night he found him.

Concerning the mystery, nothing is cleared up yet. Dad says suicide is easier for him to accept because murder might have been prevented. He believes nothing could have changed Don's mind if he decided to "finish himself." I don't know what to think. How about you? Any ideas?

Tomorrow morning a coroner's jury meets to determine the cause of death. Dad has been subpoenaed. At 11:00 they'll read the will. We already know Dad's going to get a farm or two, one of which is 800 acres. Don's employees will get $500 for each year they worked for him and, possibly, Meyer and Schmidt will also get the store—a valuable piece of real estate. Since Dad didn't have a chance to see codicils to the will, there may be more. I'll know tomorrow.

Gradually, the shock of Don's death is wearing off, but the loss will be intensified every Sunday, holiday, vacation, hunting season. The folks will adjust, although I can't imagine who Dad will hunt pheasants with. He doesn't even trust local hunters who should know how to handle guns.

If Liz can arrange it at work, we'd like to take a summer trip with Mom and Dad—a distraction for them—to Mexico, maybe.

I didn't get a letter today—a terrible blow— but maybe tomorrow? Write often and much, about anything.

Love, Marty

Chapter Six

Inquest and Will

On Thursday morning CB left for the inquest alone. Marty stayed home because Liz convinced Ellen to stay home. The sisters agreed Mom needed a break. CB's obsessing over Don's death added to her stress, evident in the dark circles under her eyes, her tendency to tear up. While Liz helped in the kitchen and talked about returning to Chicago, Marty sat down at the piano. She started slowly with the *Prelude in C*, easy Bach, to get warmed up. She tried the *Inventions* next, but her fingers weren't up to it, the left hand struggling to keep up with the right.

"Play Mozart, the *Sonata in A* . . . or *B flat*," Liz called from the kitchen.

"I don't know. My fingers are rusty." But she located the sonata book in the bench and decided on the *A Major* opening theme with less demanding finger work and timing than the Bach *Inventions*. Briefly, she felt good. Liz's attention was almost as gratifying as the playing. No question: in this area Marty surpassed her sister. Not innately, she reminded herself. She enjoyed playing and stuck with it.

By the time Marty completed the sonata, stumbling through the last movement, the *Alla Turca*, she decided to give her out-of-practice fingers a rest. She moved into the living room and looked over the three available magazines: *Readers' Digest, Field and Stream* and *House Beautiful*. Picking up the *Readers' Digest*, she turned to Liz, whose head was buried in a newspaper. "We can't blame our intellectual pretensions on our parents."

"Obviously." Liz looked up for a brief moment. Marty was reading about an "unforgettable character" when CB burst through the front door. Fresh from the coroner's jury and the reading of the will, he rushed toward the kitchen and his wife, ignoring his daughters. They put down their reading and followed.

"Well, Ellen, you got your wish, a new house. Don left his house to me." Marty felt the impact of words CB seemed to hurl at his wife. *Is he angry?* Ellen wanted a new house as long as Marty could remember, and CB said they could not afford one. No matter how much Ellen complained, CB remained firm.

"You mean the college didn't get it?" Ellen asked. They all assumed the local college would inherit the large, brick house with the highly prized Circassian walnut woodwork and multi-hued, pastel slate roof—perfect for a college president. Marty knew her mother loved it, a gift that poignantly signified Don's regard for her.

"What will you do with it?"

"Liz!" Marty scowled at her insensitive sister. "You deserve it Mom," Marty put her arms around her mother. "All the concern over the years, nursing Nellie in Minnesota, all the meals you served Don. But I'll bet it was the apple pies you made for the hunting trips that clinched it." Marty's effort at humor failed to lighten her father's mood.

"The house is big enough for us and him," CB said, shaken by this unexpected prize. "He could have deeded it to me and lived with us, if he wanted us to live there."

"Any other surprises, Dad?" Liz probed. "What did the jury decide?"

"No decision yet on the death. They meet tomorrow, and Monday they'll search the house again, more thoroughly this time if no one has come forward with information about the money. There is some new information. The younger Sterns boy came by on Saturday."

"That's Jimmy, Eric's brother. He's awfully young," Marty quickly tried to calculate how old her former classmate's brother would be.

"He's twelve now. Old enough," CB added. "He said no one answered the door when he stopped by at 1:30 to see about shoveling the walk. He also saw an old gray car parked in front of the house. So far, we don't know who that car belongs to."

"The plot thickens. I suppose it's possible the owner was in the house with Don?" Liz speculated. "But parking in such a public place doesn't make sense if you're up to no good."

"Yes, but snow made parking difficult on the side streets. Anyway, when they searched the house Monday, they didn't find any evidence Don had a visitor. They even checked the garbage looking for a clue that someone besides Don had eaten there."

"What about the neighbors Hal said got into the house?" Marty questioned. "Maybe one of them found the money and took it."

"No, Marty. Those neighbors are good people."

"Dad, you're too trusting." Liz shook her head.

As he paced, CB continued, "It seems unlikely Don left the house that day. No one saw anyone else come or go either, but what if someone came before sunrise and left after dark? Another strange thing . . . the window shades were drawn all day. At least they were down when the Stern boy was there. I don't remember Meyer mentioning it. Normally, Don didn't even pull the shades at night."

"I guess if you were planning a suicide, you might do things differently. I mean, he did stay home from work, he did send Meyer on an unusual errand," Liz said. "But I lean toward suicide, because I can't believe anyone would kill for $9,500."

"People have killed for less. To our generation $9,500 is a lot of money," Ellen added, reluctant to accept the suicide theory until CB did. "And they could have taken other valuables in the house."

"That's a new idea. Maybe $9,500 was only part of the loot." Marty expanded on this possibility. "Nellie had valuable jewelry, I'm sure, and I'll bet Don kept plenty of cash, maybe even gold coins, hidden somewhere. Didn't he have lots of guns and rifles, Dad?"

"He had several guns. I don't know who checked them on Monday. But how could they know what was missing? I don't even know exactly what he had. He probably did have gold stashed away. When you've seen crops dry up, the earth blow away, banks close like they did here in the '20s and '30s, saving a little something under the mattress, if you have it to save, is prudent. But I think most of Don's liquid assets were in his safety deposit boxes. They were stuffed."

CB's comments evoked some of Marty's earliest memories. She would never forget the Depression—the hobos coming to the house asking for food and Ellen feeding them on the back porch—or the frightening dust storms that created midnight darkness at noon by whipping up clouds of earth. She tried to escape the grit that stung her eyes by running into the house. She helped her mother close all the windows and later clean up the dirt that sifted in anyway onto the sills. She remembered the abandoned, falling-down farm houses; the Russian thistles blowing across the barren fields until trapped in old barbed wire fences; arrowheads exposed on the desolate countryside.

Eventually, the rains came and the land began to recover in the late '30s. Marty, a young teenager, went hunting occasionally with her father and Don. Their surrogate bird dog, she walked toward the two men from the opposite end of a cornfield, scaring up pheasants as she went. She loved the outdoors on those bright, brisk, November days, the dried cornstalks, the smell of fall in the air, even more than she hated to see the birds drop from the sky, felled by shot. Both men, excellent shots, usually went home with their limit. The beautiful birds lay in a heap in the back shed until Ellen got to them. Whatever they did not eat or give away, Ellen canned. Marty never liked pheasant, fresh or canned, probably because she watched her mother skin and eviscerate the birds—a messy and smelly procedure. And she hated biting into shot, which happened frequently.

"Another thing." CB broke through Marty's musings. "Why did Don address the note to CB? He always called me Charles."

Liz continued playing devil's advocate, "Dad, he didn't know who would find the note, so he addressed you the way most people do."

"The handwriting is being analyzed to be certain Don wrote it." CB suddenly stopped short. "I can't believe I forgot to tell you this. One of Don's codicils leaves each of you girls $10,000— no strings attached—in addition to the $3,500 from Nellie's will that has to be spent on education or an annuity."

Marty sat down. "Now I can go for another degree!" *How will this affect my relationship with Rich?* "Liz, what will you do with your money?"

"Invest it, probably. Anything else, Dad?"

"He left more to his employees—another codicil—$1,000 for each year of employment. And the store and stock to Bob Meyer and Jim Schmidt equally."

Richard's first letter, written on Monday, the night Marty and Liz spent in Minneapolis, arrived that afternoon. Hearing from him, reading about the minutiae of his typical day comforted Marty, though his work in the lab seemed irrelevant now. Briefly, she escaped the distress around her, but her wish to return to Chicago intensified.

"By the way, Liz, I heard you on the phone earlier. When do you leave?"

"Saturday morning. Gives me one day to recover before I go back to work."

"Is it hard to leave before the mystery is resolved?"

"No. You'll keep me informed. Anyway, in my mind the only mystery is the money, and I bet he stashed it away somewhere or delivered it that afternoon, maybe during the time he didn't answer the doorbell."

"But no one has come forward."

"Is Mom or Dad around?" Liz whispered. "I don't want them to hear me."

"No. They went somewhere together."

"I'm guessing Don had a woman and she's embarrassed; maybe she's married. I know Dad doesn't think so, but maybe he missed it because he didn't suspect it. Anyway, Dad spent most of the week in Pierre. He wasn't even around. You know, I always thought of Don as celibate—even asexual—when I thought about it, if I ever did—the way kids think of their parents—or try not to think of their parents as sexual. Didn't you?"

Marty hesitated, "I guess so. If I thought about it, I assumed Dad thought Don was celibate. And how could Dad be wrong? But you know, if it's possible he had a woman, it's possible he had a man. Do you think he was homosexual?"

"Maybe, I hadn't thought of that before. He didn't have stereotypical characteristics, but we know that's irrelevant. Interesting no one has suggested it."

"You're kidding. This is the Bible belt. No one suggested he had a woman, only that he might have wanted to help someone out financially. Homosexuality is too far out for this town—to talk about publicly anyway. And Don was, or seemed to be, a very proper Victorian."

"You know, Marty, we're making a case for extortion or blackmail. I know Dad's mentioned it. What if Don had been paying somebody off? He got tired of it and was threatening to expose the blackmailer? That's a motive for murder—beyond the money. But why, then, did he write a suicide note?"

"Stalling for time, maybe. I guess if a gun were pointed at your head, you'd do anything. You wouldn't just say, 'Go ahead, shoot.' You'd start writing, hoping something would happen. The phone would ring. The doorbell."

"Maybe," Liz agreed. "But if someone was in the house threatening him, why didn't he let Meyer know—or Dad, when he called."

"Not so easy if there's a gun pointed at you. Maybe he tried to send messages. We don't really know what he said to Meyer or Dad. It's possible they missed something."

"But not likely, Marty," Liz said, glancing at her watch. "How about joining me? I'm off to see Miss Crane. Mom says she has cancer."

"Sorry. You were the teacher's pet, not me. Anyone else you'll look up, any of your friends still around?"

"I'm not sure. Depends on how I feel tomorrow. How about you?"

"I'll call Cathy at some point. She may be the only close friend in town. And Mary Alice."

As soon as Liz returned from visiting her high school teacher, CB asked his daughters to come with him to see their grandmother. As before, this tiny, shriveled, inarticulate woman, lost in a maze of tangled brain cells, twisted her bed clothes and mumbled inaudibly. Suddenly, she seemed to find her way out of a dense fog, to find a clear voice and certitude, "I guess I'm going to die now." Instinctively, Marty reached for her father. She suppressed an impulse to give false hope, to deny her grandmother's declaration.

When they were outside, climbing into the car, Liz whispered to her sister, "Do deaths come in threes?"

"Liz, I can't believe you're superstitious."

Returning home, they found Jessie waiting with Ellen. She had stopped by and Ellen invited her to stay for dinner. During the meal, Marty wanted to prod her. *Tell us you have it. Tell us he sent you the money.* But Marty said nothing and Jessie said nothing. Ellen reported two more crank calls, the only news. Toward the end of the meal, Ellen talked about moving into the Wagner house. She turned to her daughters, "By the way girls, I want you to sort through your stuff in the attic, decide what you want to keep. Liz, you need to do it tomorrow, since you're leaving Saturday."

"Ellen," CB interjected, "Don't rush us into this. If nothing is found next Monday, I might consider moving to Don's. Maybe that's what he wanted. We'd have time to do a thorough search."

Writing to Rich that night, Marty told him about the house and the codicils. Too tired to do much more, she concluded:

> Until the mystery is solved, everyone will be up in the air. To date, I've been very busy (and tomorrow I get to clean out the attic!) but I think of you almost constantly, and I too carry on conversations. Absence may make the heart grow fonder. Write again soon and love me.
>
> I love you.
> Marty

Chapter Seven

Exploring the Attic

"God, it's cold in here. We need snow suits." Liz surveyed the stacks of cardboard cartons. "I suppose we could drag this stuff out of here."

"I'll go get jackets," Marty offered. "We'll need something while we figure out which boxes to sort through."

When Marty returned, Liz was moving from one box to another, checking the contents. "I don't think I want any of this junk. Mom saved our report cards, high school newspapers, term papers, yearbooks. Oh good, toss me that jacket."

"How would you like some Brenda Starr paper dolls?" Marty had just discovered one of her childhood collections. "Seriously, you might want to check the high school papers for some of your prize-winning articles. I intend to keep my yearbooks. In twenty or thirty years it will be fun to look back."

"Remember finding these after the dust storms?" Liz held a small carton of arrowheads.

"Finding them was fun, but walking through those barren fields . . . thank God, that's over. Remember how dry it was?

51

You could literally walk across the lake on cracked, caked earth. And Dad measuring rainfall in fractions of an inch? 'We got one-one hundredth of an inch of rain today!' How many drops do you think that was?"

"I guess we need to save them. They might have historical value. We assumed they were Sioux, but they could be much older than that. Oh, look what I found." Liz bent over a black, rectangular case.

"Grandpa's ashes," Marty exclaimed. "When I was little, that black case really scared me—even though I never believed in ghosts."

"Does seem a little bizarre. You'd think Grandma or Dad would have buried or scattered the ashes long ago. How many years have they been here?"

"He died in 1916."

"Well, it won't be long now. I suppose he'll be buried with Grandma. How do you know he died in 1916?"

"I'm good at dates, remember?"

"Did you know he was cremated in Minnesota?" Liz read a small, yellow tag attached to the heavy case. "Can you imagine shipping a body 300 miles?"

"No. Must have been the closest crematorium. I remember Dad saying his father wanted to be cremated to be sure he wasn't buried alive."

"I guess it happened occasionally, but being burned alive doesn't exactly appeal either. Hey, let's talk about something less depressing. Tell me about Dick—I mean, Rich. Do you ever call him Dick?"

"Are you kidding? I think he'd come close to killing anyone who called him Dick."

"Why?"

"He hates Nixon with a passion, really disliked him long before the Checkers speech."

"What does Dad think of that?"

"I don't think he knows and I won't educate him. On the other hand, Dad always excused our liberal politics—yours and mine—on the grounds that we're young. He still thinks we'll smarten up when we grow up."

"Do you think we will?"

"No. Poor Mom and Dad. We've been well-behaved, achieving daughters—daughters to be proud of—yet both of us have rejected his politics and her religion . . . what they valued most."

"I don't feel guilty. Do you?

"Sometimes."

"Anyway, I'd rather hear about you and Rich. Are you getting married? And whatever happened to Wally?"

"I don't know in either case," Marty answered. "How about you and your pilot or lawyer friends?"

"No, no. I've never been serious. I don't get into relationships like you do. You and Richard seem devoted. Are you in love?"

"I think so. I'm not sure I know what I feel—or what love is, for that matter. And even if I do love him, I'm not sure what kind of commitment I want to make. One big problem, Liz, is money. If we marry, I'd have to get a job to support him through graduate school. He still has a long way to go and his GI Bill is running out. Even with the inheritance I'm not sure how both of us could stay in school. My friend Gail gave up graduate school, but her husband is a medic. She can return eventually. Rich will never make much money as an academic. And what if I got pregnant?"

"I'm sure you've heard of birth control. But, I *do* understand. Anyway, it sounds as if Wally is definitely a fling of the past, a flame gone out."

Marty chose to ignore Liz's sarcasm. "I guess. Wally and I never really broke up, just went in different directions. I think he was joining the Navy the last time I saw him."

"Do you think it's possible to love more than one person at a time?"

"Why not? Why couldn't you love two or more people for different qualities? Rich is serious, hardworking, tenacious, curious to an extreme. Wally was more spontaneous, uninhibited, more fun—maybe. A little mysterious, a Fitzgerald character—like Gatsby. Both are smart, neither are creative in an artistic sense, especially, although Rich is inventive, a good problem solver." Marty stopped, momentarily out of adjectives.

"I think you made a better case for Rich."

"I know, but Wally had something I can't quite capture in words. Of course, I didn't know him like I know Richard. We were only in high school, and he was the first boy who noticed me."

"Didn't happen to me in high school."

"How about Frank Sumner? Seems to me that was a serious crush."

"Very short lived. I don't think I ever want to marry. Cooking, cleaning, waiting on a man, babies. Not for me."

"No? Sometimes I'm tempted. Gail and Bill seem happy and I kinda like their lifestyle." As Marty reorganized the contents of cartons, she set aside yearbooks and a stack of letters. When Ellen called, announcing the mail, Marty stood and stretched, eager to take a break.

"Better hurry," Liz taunted. "You must have a letter from Rich."

"You're just jealous," Marty laughed. *How often have we thrown that line at each other?*

Marty found Rich's letter on a table near the front door. The letter was short and complaining. He hadn't heard from her. He promised to write more the next day if he got a letter. Annoyed, she wondered why the mail was so slow. When she counted the days, though, his petulance seemed unreasonable, if flattering. *He must really miss me.* She was rereading the letter when Liz walked into the room.

"I can only take so much ancient history. Oh, oh. You look perplexed. Trouble in paradise?"

"Liz, do you think Mom or Dad would care if I called Rich?"

"Of course not. I think they like him. And think what a relief if you married him."

"Seriously, Liz, cut the sarcasm."

"Sarcastic or not, don't you think they'd love to have us both married off? Isn't that what most parents want for their daughters?"

"I suppose, but your Pollyanna sister also believes they want us to be happy. So you think it's okay to call Rich since it furthers the parental goal?"

"Just call."

Having Liz's approval made a difference. Now all Marty needed was to find a time when she could talk in private and catch Rich at home—probably after evening guests departed. Tonight several guests were expected, including Don's cousins.

Hal's arrival after dinner with a bottle of Scotch and wine "for the ladies" ushered in a party atmosphere, an elevation of mood Marty hoped would last beyond the evening.

Conversation swirled around the report of another car, supposedly parked on Saturday near the small garage toward the back of Don's property, and the impending search of the house by the coroner's jury. Because CB knew Don and the house better than anyone on the jury, he was invited to join the search. The jury also decided to hire a private detective. Marty was considering how this would impact her parents when the phone rang.

Liz took the call and motioned to Marty a few seconds later. Marty excused herself from the group and joined Liz. "It's Rich, worried about you," she said with a knowing smile. Marty took the phone and waited until Liz rejoined the group in the living room.

"Hi, what a wonderful surprise. You won't believe this, but I was going to call you tonight."

"Too bad, I should have waited. I'm relieved you're not annoyed. I haven't received any mail, and I was beginning to wonder."

"What? I've written tomes every day. I'm the laughing stock around here," she exaggerated. "You know, I didn't get here until Tuesday and this is only Friday. What can you expect from the Pony Express? You'll probably get two letters tomorrow."

"I hope. It's lonely here without you. Everything okay?"

"Oh, yes and no. There's so much, too much to discuss over the phone, but I did write long letters. I'm eager to hear your views on Don's death. Money is still missing, so nothing is resolved. Before I forget, did you talk to my instructors?"

"Yes, except for Bettelheim. You're getting two Incompletes and Dr. Martin says the job will keep. They're looking for new funding and rethinking the direction of the research anyway. Did you know that? You may be involved in writing a new research proposal."

"Sounds interesting and challenging. Do you think Bettelheim will be difficult?"

"They don't call him Brutalheim for nothing! Just kidding. No, I haven't caught up with him yet."

"By the way, I have good news. I'm going to inherit some money. I think, $13,500. You can help me figure out how to use it."

"That should be easy!"

"Thirty-five hundred has to be used for education, so I can stay in school. Oh I have something more urgent." Marty turned her back toward the living room, alive with talk, even occasional laughter. "I'm sure I told you that Dad is diabetic."

"Yeah, we talked about it once."

"Well, he's controlled it in the past, but now his urine has sugar whenever he tests it. There are other problems too. Could you find out from Bill the procedure for being admitted to Billings Hospital and the cost of a checkup? I figure Mom and Dad could stay with me for a few weeks while one, or both, get thorough physicals. I might get back to Chicago sooner, if I can convince them to do it."

"Sure. I'll talk to Bill. Do you know when they would come?"

"No, unfortunately, Dad won't leave Grandma right now. She's really pathetic, Rich, and I don't think she'll last much longer. Anyway I'll start working on Dad in earnest when I have more information. He may be hard to convince, but Mom will do whatever he wants."

"I'll see Bill this weekend. Any idea how much longer you'll be there?"

"Not really. Liz leaves tomorrow. Rich, this call is getting expensive and I should go back to the guests, anyway. I'm glad you called. I'll call you soon."

"Don't worry about the cost. My nickel. I'm leading a frugal life. I miss you. I love you."

"Bye. Look for my letters tomorrow and write." Checking again to be sure no one was within earshot, Marty said softly, "I love you, too. I can hardly wait to get back there."

"Hang in there, sweetie. Bye."

Guests were leaving when Marty returned to the living room. When they were gone, she helped Ellen and Liz collect the empty glasses and half-filled bowls and plates of chips and cheese.

"Was that Rich, dear?" Ellen asked.

"Yeah, he wondered about registering me for courses next quarter."

"He's a nice young man. I did feel bad for Carl, though, when you broke up."

Liz must be right. Mom wants me to get married. "I thought Wally was your favorite." For a moment Marty could see Wally kneeling before Ellen and her mother's coquettish response.

"I did like Wally—he was a charmer—but that was so long ago. And I like Richard too. Oh, why don't we sit in the kitchen and have coffee and cake? This is Liz's last night."

Sitting around the kitchen table late at night was a family ritual Marty enjoyed. As a child, she felt privileged to be present for parental discussions of politics, her father's consuming passion. Now, they talked about politics and Liz's work in Chicago. CB still hoped his older child—the one who should have been a boy—would become a lawyer, would succeed in the profession he deemed the best preparation for a political career. But neither Liz nor Marty, despite their admiration of Jessie, had ever been interested in law or politics as a career. Marty wondered if Liz believed her father was disappointed in her sex and if she resented it, especially since she fulfilled most of his expectations.

Marty often felt her parents expected less of her, yet Mom pushed dance lessons, piano lessons, even voice lessons. Marty dug in her heels on the first and last, although later she regretted not taking tap. Were Ellen's stage-mother tendencies the result of her own sense of inferiority, her unhappiness and occasional self-pity because she never had these opportunities? Was her mother's dissatisfaction a driving force in Marty's life? Unconscious, of course. Had her father, with an advanced degree, been less influential than her mother without even a high school diploma? Possibly, but Marty also believed her need to compete with Liz, to explore, to experience, to achieve, to accomplish derived, in part, from her own internal chemistry.

Lost in thought, Marty sat quietly while Liz talked about her job. When Liz said she needed to pack and get to bed, Marty followed her upstairs. This might be her last chance to talk to Liz alone for a long time. Once upstairs, however, she talked idly about packing. "I know I should be asking you weighty questions, but my mind is a blank," she said.

"You'll be fine," Liz said. "The worst is over."

"I hope."

Liz wanted an unemotional exit, a cab to the airport alone, but both CB and Ellen insisted on taking her. Under these circumstance, she wanted Marty as buffer. *Not fair. Where will she be when I need her?* But Marty liked getting out into the countryside, experiencing the snow-covered prairie sparkling in the sunlight. As much as she wanted to return to Chicago, she did not miss the endless blocks of brick apartment buildings that often propelled her toward the Midway or Lake Michigan where the open space allowed her to breath more easily.

After Liz's plane took off, CB said he wanted to visit his mother before they returned home. "She'll be 92 in just one month."

"Born during the Civil War," Marty added. "Seems so long ago—another century."

"She's had a good life, except for the last few months. She was blessed with good health and healthy children and grandchildren." Ellen turned toward Marty in the back seat, "And she was a good mother-in-law to me."

"What about her childhood, though?" Marty asked. "I remember her telling me about a stepmother straight out of *Grimm's Fairy Tales.*"

"It's true," CB acknowledged. "She was only six when her mother died, and her father left her with relatives in the east. Later he remarried and took her to Chicago where she graduated from a small finishing school."

"That's where she learned to play piano." Marty visualized her grandmother at the piano, playing the one piece she remembered.

"Yes. And when she was 19 or 20, her father talked her and her brother into homesteading in Dakota Territory."

"And she lived alone in a sod hut to claim the land." Marty loved this story.

"In one sense she wasn't alone. Her father and brother were doing the same thing not far away."

"Well, I can't imagine living through a Dakota winter in a hut by myself," Marty said. "I'd die of fright if the elements didn't get me. Think of the wind and snow. You could get buried alive." Reminiscing about her grandmother's past renewed Marty's reverence for this now fragile, once intrepid, woman.

When they arrived, Marty braced herself as they entered the small house. *How sad her life ends in this ruinous descent into death.* As Marty bent over to kiss her grandmother's forehead, she wondered if this pathetic figure figured in Don's death. Did Don worry about having a stroke and decide to quit life while he was ahead? She looked around. Six other women in three rooms were bedridden like her grandmother. Were they all pioneers too?

On the way home Marty, preoccupied with her grandparents' past, asked CB about his father. "Did he homestead too?"

"He came to Dakota Territory from Wisconsin to publish a newspaper, but moved on to manage the local land office. Your grandmother's father was a printer, so my father hired his future father-in-law to print the paper he put together. It worked well—for me anyway. My parents got married soon after, in 1882, I think."

"Any problems with Indians in those days?" Marty asked, aware her education mostly neglected the native part of Dakota history. She knew there were several reservations in South Dakota but not much else.

"Not around here. The uprisings were west of the Missouri mostly—Wounded Knee, for one. Ask your mother. She grew up in the Black Hills, sacred land to the Sioux."

"Mom?"

"All I remember is that nice young ladies stayed away from Lead and Deadwood. A wild bunch hung out in those towns, drinking and gambling and shooting too. But I don't remember problems with Indians especially."

"You didn't know your mother hung out with Wild Bill and Calamity Jane," CB joshed.

"Oh, for heavens sake, Charles."

"It's okay, Mom, I know you're not that old!" Marty said reassuringly, surprised her mother, after all these years, could still feel picked-on. For Marty the kidding meant the twinkle in her father's eye was beginning to return.

Home again, Marty decided to write to Rich in spite of CB's tease about "another letter to Richard." Dad's really doing better, she decided, as she lit a cigarette and started writing about her grandmother, the guests of the previous evening, and the continuing mystery.

There are no additional clues and no sign of the money, but we're still hoping someone will come forward. When the house is searched again on Monday, Dad will be there. I think he is closer to accepting Don's death as suicide. He's even beginning to seem more like his old self, although he looked stricken when his *Field and Stream* came today.

Did I mention that Liz and I tried to convince the folks to have Jessie over a lot to help her get through this period, because she has taken Don's death pretty badly? Fortunately, she is very active and has many interests. Like Don, she appears to be healthy, although she has the beginnings of Parkinson's Disease. So far, it hasn't slowed her down any.

Talk about the house continues. Dad says if Don wanted him to live in the house, he shouldn't have killed himself there. Still, I think he will succumb to pressure from Mom to move, so he can continue the search for the money (unless it shows up soon.)

Sometimes I feel so bad for Dad. Did I ever tell you that he enlisted in the Great War because he felt someone in the family should? He was over 30. He claims his hair turned white in the '20s because local banks failed and he worried about Grandma's and his own financial losses. Things got worse in the '30s during the Depression. He lost his job as postmaster when Roosevelt became president. He was a Republican long before that—actually a LaFollette Republican originally. He was speaker of the South Dakota House of Representatives before the army.

Enough family history. I miss you more every day. I'm still hoping to get back before the end of the quarter, possibly with the folks. I keep trying to convince Dad he needs to think about his own health.

I hope my letters are finally arriving. I do take some razzing for being so faithful. My parents like you. Mom was very clear about that last night.

Keep writing and loving me,
Marty

Chapter Eight

Richard's Obsession

Richard began looking for mail from Marty and composing letters to her the day after she left. To comply with her wishes he approached two of her instructors the next day and asked for Incompletes. He also worked in the psychology shop, improving equipment for testing the parameters of flicker fusion, and ran two subjects before he went home to eat. In the evening he read, wrote to his folks and the short complaining letter to Marty. He mentioned his meeting with her instructors and stressed his eagerness to hear from her, trying not to sound like a nag.

Around noon on Wednesday he rushed to his apartment, hoping to find a letter from her. No luck. No mail on Thursday, either. *I'm as bad off as the rats, pacing in their cages, waiting for food pellets. Only they're luckier than I am.* Both nights, unable to suppress his disappointment, he wrote a short note, with apologies in case she had written. He did not write on Friday, but late in the evening he decided to make the phone call. It was okay. She actually seemed pleased.

When he found two letters and the post card from Minneapolis in the mail on Saturday, he felt slightly foolish, then guilty, and, finally, angry the mail was so slow. But the mystery of the money intrigued him and he quickly enumerated several thoughts off the top of his head:

1) Don't fly back.
2) Why was Meyer at the hotel with Erickson? Was he going to meet with Don and Erickson?
3) If Don was planning suicide, his behavior seems strange—calling to say he'd keep an appointment that he knew he wouldn't keep.
4) Saying he'd be over to your place the next day.
5) He certainly wouldn't send $50 and $100 bills in the mail and he evidently didn't go to the PO to register a letter or send a money order. Bills of that denomination are handy for a pay-off. They'll be hard to trace if someone really did extort them, which seems likely in view of the fact that they're in 50 and 100 denominations.
6) Don must have needed light after 6:00 p.m. to get around the house, to write the suicide note, etc. If the house was dark when your parents arrived, who turned off the lights?
6) Don's empathy with your father regarding your grandmother makes his inability to talk to him somewhat feasible—except that . . .
8) Then it's hard to understand why he would burden someone already burdened by committing suicide and leaving that note without realizing the effect on the person he didn't want to trouble.

So much for that. I'm not a sleuth—just that I noted several inconsistencies as I read your account. They probably iron out when one knows the whole story.

Honey, about trying to divert your folks. A certain amount of remorse is necessary. What I mean is—don't worry too much if your parents seem distraught. Don't try to invent escapes for awhile. I'm sure there is some therapeutic value in all of it. I don't think you're not justified in concern over your parents. Just consider your own chaotic emotional state right now.

Spence just called and wants me to come over for coffee. Bill and Gail will be there. I'll let Gail know how you're doing and I'll find out how she is. Let me know if you want me to tell Bettelheim something special and should I register you for next quarter? Will send you the *Maroon* and *Chi Review* tomorrow.

I Love You, Bushel and a Peck
Rich

As he walked to Spence's, Richard congratulated himself for not writing about love as a neurosis or his reasons for rejecting Plato and Socrates ideas on love. When he arrived at Spence's apartment, he found George, Bill, and Gail sitting at the kitchen table, drinking coffee and eating Oreos. Spence was putting a record on his turntable. Richard poured himself a cup of coffee and pulled up a chair next to Bill.

"What have you heard from Marty?" Gail asked.

"Well, the nature of the death is still in question." Richard told them as much as he knew.

"I'll bet a woman is involved, someone he didn't want to acknowledge publicly or embarrass by putting in his will," Bill suggested.

"Maybe he was homosexual and paying off a man," George countered. "That would make coming forward even more difficult, whether legitimate or blackmail."

"They're possibilities, I suppose. Marty characterized Don as having no bad habits. Midwestern, Puritanical denial, maybe. Her father thinks someone may have been in the house demanding payment. And that could mean extortion, blackmail, or just simple robbery."

"How's Marty doing?" Gail asked.

"Okay, I think. It's been rough, especially for her parents. She worries about them. How are you? You look good."

"Gaining too much weight. But I feel good except for getting tired."

"Speaking of tired, we'd better get you home," Bill interrupted. "Before you fall asleep and I have to carry you."

"Spence, I should go too . . . after you tell me about that music. It's beautiful. Marty would love it."

"I'm sure Marty knows Schuman's *Piano Concerto in A Minor*. But she might not know this recording with Dinu Lipatti as pianist."

"You're probably right. Thanks for the coffee. See you tomorrow."

Back at his apartment rereading his mail from Marty, Richard realized Liz should be home. He found the phone number Marty gave him before she left and called Liz without much care for the time.

"She's fine, Rich," Liz said reassuringly. "I'm sure she wrote you about the missing money. It was still missing when I left. Look, Rich, I'm exhausted. I need to unpack and get to bed. Marty was so faithful about writing, you'll get a stack of letters soon. Anyway, call me Monday night. It will be good to talk. I can fill you in on any details Marty missed."

Although disappointed by their brief conversation, Richard was not surprised. He and Liz never had much to say to each other. Just as well. He'd start another letter to Marty.

Dear Marty,

I'm still two people: the one who talks to you and the one who talks to others—at the same time. I really felt it tonight at Spence's, reporting to them some of what you wrote to me. Maybe it disproves the old axiom (two people in the same place, same time). One of the worst things about the whole day is coming home alone, knowing I won't see you later. I can't sleep unless I'm real tired. I put off going to bed as long as possible.

Gail asked about you tonight. I'm happy to report that she's gaining weight. I think she looks good, healthy for a change. She always was too skinny. She seems really proud to be pregnant. She pats her belly a lot and wears maternity clothes (which I don't think she needs yet.)

My letters must seem trivial to you. I don't feel comfortable writing much about Don, etc. because I'm sure I can't see things clearly from here, so I focus on the little things I'd tell you if you were here.

For example, I forgot to mention this good news: The landlady came to your building with a teenager yesterday. He whitewashed the basement walls. Almost looks like a hospital down there. She even washed and swept the floors. Real nice. Wish you were here. Scenery is beautiful!

I don't look forward to tomorrow, because it's Sunday. I'll have to get out of this lonely place. I'm sorry. Tomorrow will probably be bad for you too.

One more thought: Maybe we should spend next quarter studying for finals, get them out of the way before summer. Did I mention, I've actually started filling out applications for doctoral study elsewhere? I'm trying to decide who should write letters of recommendation. When it comes right down to it, I don't really want to leave here unless you come with me. But, as you know, my GI Bill runs out next quarter and I have to find funding.

Honey, I hope things are settling down there. Please try to be detached from time to time, to get above it all and look down at yourself and others involved. That helps sometimes. It's what a dialectician (or scientist or even artist) must do. I've been thinking about Hemingway's definition of courage—grace under pressure. I guess you all have that, more than I do.

I will go to bed shortly where I will talk to you until I fall asleep. I guess I worry that you do not miss me.

I love you very much (too much?)
Rich

When Richard heard the wind—*March coming in like a lion*—he dragged himself out of bed. With no experiments scheduled today, he could do whatever he wanted. Unknowingly, he began to hum "Saturday Night is the Loneliest Night of the Week." When it registered, he decided Sunday was worse—no mail. He could walk over to Readers Drug Store, mail his letter in the box outside, buy the Sunday *Times* or the *Tribune*, and go to Marty's to read it. Or he could eat breakfast or lunch at Readers, maybe bump into someone. But before he did anything, he decided to add to last night's letter:

Honey, If I can help you in any way, if there is anything I can do, please let me know. I wish you'd call me collect when your parents aren't present. I really miss you. I love you and I think you love me too . . . I hope anyway. There is no pleasure, only pain, for me in being separated from you. Maybe, the reason I'm not like most American males in this regard is that it is you I'm separated from and not just a girlfriend in the usual sense. Maybe we're an unhealthy pair (or me at least). I think Simmel said only two real strong individuals could enjoy(?) true love. Do you remember what I'm referring to? Part of an essay on social sanctions (about honor, etc.).

I hope you miss me as much as I miss you, only not so painfully.

Wish I were a poet instead of a nag!

Your Honey

Richard checked the pick-up times before he dropped his letter into the mailbox. He was thinking about killing the day by searching for the box with the earliest pickup when Bill walked out of the drug store.

"Hey, what are you doing out this early on Sunday?"

"I needed to pick up something for Gail's stomach."

"Don't you get that stuff free at Billings?"

"Usually, but I'm off today and this is the first time she's needed anything."

"Bill, I need to talk to you about Marty's father. Do you have time for a cup of coffee?"

"Not now. Gail's waiting. Why don't you come up to the apartment?"

"Are you sure it's okay"

"Oh sure. It's just morning sickness. Saltines didn't work."

When they got to the apartment, Gail was feeling better. She made coffee and toast, apologizing for not frying eggs. "Some smells really get to me."

As they ate, Richard told them about Marty's wish to have her father admitted to Billings for a thorough physical. "Bill, can you help?"

"That won't be a problem. Give me some advance notice and I can take care of it. The cost will be reasonable."

"Now that you guys have settled that, how about a Bogart double feature on 63rd street?"

"Great idea, Gail." Richard couldn't resist, although he knew he'd miss not having Marty to rehash and discuss casting choices afterwards. "I can't think of a better way to get through a long Sunday afternoon."

By the time they left the theatre, 63rd Street had come alive. Richard, trying to be heard above the noise of street traffic and the elevated train, shouted, "Let's get a Spanish omelet at cheap Alexanders."

Between El trains, Gail asked, "I've heard people talk about 'cheap Alexanders.' Why is it called that?"

"There's two Alexanders. This is the only one students can afford. I discovered it long ago and introduced Marty. She loves their Spanish omelets, so we usually come here when we eat out together. If somebody else cooks them, will the eggs be okay for you?"

"I think so. I'll give it a try anyway."

All three were eating omelets when Pete, fresh from a sculpture exhibit at the Art Institute, walked into the restaurant and joined them. When they'd finished dinner, Bill and Gail decided to leave. Richard and Pete lingered over a second cup of coffee and dessert to discuss the exhibit, Bogart films and great directors—Ford, Huston, Welles, Hitchcock—until Richard noticed the time. "Pete, I've got to go to the lab and then stop by Marty's apartment."

Richard left Pete on 63rd Street and walked down Greenwood toward the Midway. The illuminated TV screens he saw through darkened windows reminded him of *Prufrock*. He imagined silver heads of lonely old people fixated on the screen, a pathetic replacement for their losses. He hurried on—grateful he was young and his loss only temporary.

When he got to Marty's much later, Richard felt close to her. Snug in her lair and surrounded by her possessions, he wanted to hold her, to love her—a need he could only partly satisfy by writing. This time he would tell her about his conversation with Bill, the films he saw, and meeting Pete. He ended:

> I'm so glad the Korean thing is coming to an end. I dread the thought of ever going back into the army, mainly because of the separation. How do couples do it? What's with them? Some married people spend at least half their time apart— salesmen, servicemen, important people—and actually do so voluntarily—to make more money. It's barbarian!!
>
> Here's looking at you kid! (Nothing so good in the movies today.)
>
> Bushel and a Peck
> Rich

When he finished, Richard turned off the lights and lay down on the sofa. Snowflakes, illuminated by a streetlight, drifted gently past the window. *Snowing again; at least it's March.* He was asleep in seconds.

Chapter Nine

Old Friends

Marty missed Liz—a key element in her sense of belonging in this setting—an unexpected discovery. She wandered aimlessly around the house like a tumbleweed blown about on the prairie, no longer rooted. For brief periods the piano stabilized her, as a fence held the weed. Initially, she played the familiar Mozart and Bach. As her technique improved, she tackled the *Pathetique*, often doubting her hands and skill were big enough for Beethoven sonatas, but also believing she needed to push the limits to grow. Between episodes at the piano, she read *Anna Karenina*.

On Sunday, Ellen woke Marty. "How long has it been since you've gone to church? Not counting the funeral."

"Oh, Mom. I don't know. It's been a while."

"Even your Dad goes sometimes. He'd love to have you join us today."

"Okay. I'll be downstairs in a few minutes."

Sitting in church, Marty marveled at her father's "conversion." She remembered parental arguments around his church attendance, his excuses—he had to shovel the walk, take out ashes, cut the grass—although he supported Ellen in sending the children to Sunday school. She could not remember a serious discussion about religion with him, although a comment that Jesus, Mohammed, Confucius and others were all great men probably planted the first seeds of doubt in her Christian beliefs.

In junior and senior high school Marty went to church with friends for social reasons. She rarely focused on the sermon. Today, she thought about the phone calls she'd decided to make to Cathy and Mary Alice later that afternoon.

Mary Alice arrived for coffee the next morning about half an hour later than scheduled. She had been a regular playmate during school vacations. Marty would never forget the summer Mary Alice, older and Catholic, frightened her so much about spending eternity in purgatory that she insisted Ellen have her baptized.

"Hi, Marty. Sorry I'm late. I dropped Johnny next door with my mother and she wanted to talk to me about Bobby. He's still Mom's baby."

"You could have brought Johnny with you."

"No way!"

"How is Bobby? Remember how we used to tease him, run and hide from him until he went home crying? Gosh, it's really been a long time."

"Sure has. The brat finally grew up. Bobby's going to college next fall, only because he got a basketball scholarship."

"That's terrific. Have a seat and I'll pour the coffee."

"How are you? Are you still in Chicago? Have any children?"

"I'm good. Not married. How old is your baby?"

"Johnny is 10 months. You don't know how lucky you are. I sure hope I don't have any more kids. Two are enough. Mary Margaret's not so bad. She's in first grade."

"That's about how old I was when you moved in next door. Remember dressing up in Mom's old dresses and high heels? And making paper doll clothes from old wall paper sample books?"

"And trading pictures of movie stars. I still like Alan Ladd."

"I think I like Bogart best now. Certainly not Ronald Reagan."

"Marty, I hope this isn't a touchy subject. I've been reading about Don Wagner's death in the paper. Is that why you're home?"

"Yes. It's been hard on my parents."

"I remember him parking his Cadillac in front of your house. He always had the best car in town. Is there stuff that hasn't been in the newspaper?"

"Not really." Marty shrugged, unsure of what to divulge.

Soon conversation lagged. Mary Alice had little interest in resurrecting prepubescent days—the games they played inside and out or the trouble they got into sneaking cookies from her salesman father's sample boxes.

"I really should go. Mother will be having a fit if the baby's any trouble."

"Say hello to your mother for me." Marty had felt sorry for Mary Alice when she was young, because her mother made her do lots of housework.

Marty hoped the visit with Cathy—a good friend from a later period in her life—would be better. She admired Cathy during her adolescence; a sweet, feminine girl who glided smoothly from childhood to womanhood and married a young veteran she corresponded with during the war. Marty knew through the yearly exchange of Christmas cards that they had an infant daughter and lived nearby. Although their lives diverged years ago, Marty figured they could gossip about mutual friends from school.

"Hi, Cathy." Marty expected her warm welcome, but the soiled shirt and the smell of sour milk on her once fastidious friend surprised her.

"C'mon in Marty. I'm a mess. Laura just spit up on me." She led Marty into a small kitchen. "I'm heating a bottle. If I'm lucky, she'll nap." She put Laura down in a crib with the bottle propped up and then changed her shirt. "I feel better now."

"I guess talking about the 'good old high school days' isn't exactly what's on your mind when you have a baby," Marty said.

"Just the opposite. Last night I was telling Phil about that basketball game at the Corn Palace. That was a trip. How many of us piled into one car to drive the 50 miles to Mitchell?"

"Too many. How about the tournament in Aberdeen? That was the first time I smoked a cigarette. I remember somebody told me I didn't know how to open the pack." Marty could hear the baby fussing in the bedroom.

"Excuse me." Cathy retreated to the bedroom and returned with Laura in her arms. "Have you seen Wally yet?"

"Wally?"

"Yes. Phil ran into him the other night at the Pheasant Lounge."

"I had no idea he was around. We lost touch years ago." Marty tried to sound casual. "I wonder what he's up to. Did Phil say?"

"Are you still interested?" Cathy put Laura into a jump swing.

"Oh, just curious. Wally was joining the Navy the last time I saw him."

"Don't you have a guy in Chicago?"

"Yeah. We're not engaged. I want a graduate degree before I marry."

"Well, I'm not surprised you're still in school. Marty, You were always the brainy one. But I bet you'll change your mind when you find the right guy. Remember my mother's saying, 'Every pot has a lid?'"

"I think I've found the right guy. So Phil didn't really find out much about Wally?"

"He didn't tell me anything. How serious were you about Wally? You weren't with him very long."

"We fought a lot. He was my first boyfriend and I don't think either one of us knew how to handle it. You're so vulnerable at that age. If you discover the feelings aren't mutual, you're devastated and retreat. Or you get mad and pick a fight—just another defensive, face-saving maneuver."

"What did you see in him? He wasn't especially good-looking."

"No, but he was fun. You didn't know him, because he moved to town toward the end of junior year. We shared a homeroom and his locker was next to mine. So we bumped into each other a lot."

"He *was* a good football player."

"I liked his attention. I guess he had a good line."

"Did you stay in touch after high school?"

"Not at the beginning, but he called Chicago from California one night during my first year in college. The house head in my dorm woke me around midnight and told me to come to her apartment. She thought there was a death in the family. He just called to talk. Didn't stop to think what time it was in Chicago, or didn't care. Anyway, we wrote to each other after that."

"Hey, that's romantic." Cathy picked up the fussing baby again.

"The summer after I graduated, he came to town. I thought I loved him, but we were too different. He's pleasure seeking, fun to be with, but not serious enough for me. Cathy, it's getting late. I should go."

"I'm glad you came. I'm inviting you to a baby shower in a couple of days. Hope you don't mind. So, we'll be in touch."

Although the news her father brought at dinnertime was disappointing, Marty only half attended. She was rehearsing a

76

phone call to Wally in her head and trying to anticipate his response.

"Marty, you aren't listening," CB complained as Ellen served dessert.

"I heard. You didn't find the money or any messages in Don's house. You checked the tackle box and the sleeping bag? Were all the guns there? And jewelry?"

"Yes, yes. Four of us went through that house with a fine-tooth comb. We spent hours looking. Still, there's always a possibility we missed something." CB cut into his baked apple, sweetened with saccharin, a concession to his diabetes. "God, would I love a piece of your apple pie, Ellen."

"Why would he make it so difficult," Ellen asked, "if he wanted you to find the money?"

"Maybe he didn't. A logical place to him might escape us."

"Now what?" Marty asked.

"Well, I pushed and they're definitely hiring a detective. We need a fresh mind. He can find out about that gray car on the south side of the house. Find out what crooks were in town that weekend."

"Have either of you seen Wally?" Marty asked, when CB stopped talking.

"No. Is he in town?" Ellen responded.

"According to Cathy. I'll give him a call. Maybe get to see him."

"Oh, that's nice, Marty." Ellen hesitated. "Unless Richard would mind?"

"Mother! Why should he mind? Wally is just an old friend."

"All right. I guess I'm just a little old-fashioned."

Marty got up and carried her dishes to the sink, hoping to end the conversation. She continued the cleanup until her parents disappeared into the living room. When she heard the radio, she looked for the phone book and then the Neilson's number. Standing before the black box on the wall, she reviewed her introduction before she took the receiver off the hook and dialed.

"Hi, Mrs. Neilsen. This is Marty Black. Remember me?"

"Of course. Hello stranger. It's good to hear from you."

"How are you and Mr Neilsen?"

"We're pretty good. How about you?"

"Fine. I heard that Wally is in town. Is he home?"

"Not at the moment, but he should be back soon and I know he'd love to talk to you. How late can he call?"

"Oh . . . late. I rarely go to bed before midnight."

"He should be here long before that. I'll have him give you a call."

"Okay. Thanks. Goodbye." Marty hung up, happily surprised Mrs. Neilsen remembered her.

Now the wheels were in motion. While she waited, Marty pulled *The Short Stories of Ernest Hemingway*, from the bookshelf. She hadn't finished *Anna Karenina* yet, but short stories, she decided, fit her attention span. And Wally reminded her of Hemingway—both were bigger than life. She started *A Clean, Well Lighted Place* because it was five pages long, but it was depressing with the suicidal, old man, preoccupied with "nada." When the call came, Marty stood up to let her parents know she'd answer, then let it ring four times.

"Hello."

"Marty, how are you, Babe?"

"Good, and you?"

"Eager to see you. How about going out for a drink?"

"When?"

"Now."

"It's a little late."

"What about tomorrow? Lunch?"

"I guess. I'm surprised you're home." Her mind was a jumble.

"I won't be here much longer, but we can talk about it tomorrow—unless you've changed your mind about tonight."

"No. It's late. Tomorrow is fine. Say noon or 1:00."

"I'll pick you up at noon. Still in Chicago?"

"Yes. Why did you stop writing?"

"Why did you? Hey, I'll bet you're working on a doctorate. You're not still reading Aristotle and Plato? You've got to be doing something more practical than worrying about a perfect society."

Marty laughed, "Now it's Freud and Rogers, Mead and Horney and others. Probably no more helpful than the Greeks. Actually, what would Freud have done without *Oedipus*?"

"Well, I'm more interested in your sex life. Still friendly with Carl?"

"Still friendly, but not a couple anymore."

"A new boyfriend?"

"Hey, why the third degree? How about you? Still playing the field?"

"Of course. My motto is 'Love 'em all.' I haven't changed and it doesn't sound as if you have either, although your reading list has improved."

"I don't think I've changed much, not enough, probably."

"I'll be the judge. See you tomorrow."

"Good night."

"Good night, Bright Eyes."

Marty told herself it was nothing special. She was just going to see an old friend. "Hey, do you mind if I call Rich?" Marty asked her father.

"Go ahead, honey."

"Marty, it's great to hear from you. I didn't expect it. Any news about the mystery?"

"Not much. What's going on there?"

He told her about his talks with Bill and her professors. She told him about visiting with Mary Alice and Cathy.

"I envy them." Richard said. "I miss you."

Grudgingly, Marty admired his honesty, the way he risked vulnerability. But it also made her impatient with him. Her response, that she missed him too, sounded obligatory, even to her. "I should get to bed."

"Okay, Sweetie, thanks for calling. Good night."

Before retiring, she wrote him a note, mostly about her grandmother's condition. She ended by describing Hal Mason's "retrained" Doberman, a German war dog—an animal story she knew he would like.

During the night, Marty awoke with dreams that slipped away as fast as she tried to grasp and fix them in her memory. Wally, Rich, test data, Dobermans, Chicago, *nada.*

Chapter Ten

Enter Wally

Watching Wally get out of the gray sedan and walk up to her front door, Marty began to compare: taller and heavier than Rich with a much larger frame. Both had blue eyes and sandy-colored hair, cut short. She took a deep breath before opening the door.

"Hi, Wally."

"Hi, Beautiful."

For an awkward second she thought he was going to kiss her. "Want to come in for a minute?"

"Maybe later. Have you ever eaten at the Daum Hotel?"

She slipped on her coat as she went out the door. "Not in years."

"My mother says the restaurant has a good brunch. And I'm hungry."

"You always did have a big appetite."

He winked at her as he opened the car door. "Glad you remembered."

Just like Hemingway, Marty thought, when Wally asked her if she wanted a Bloody Mary before lunch. "Too early for me."

She remembered how his drinking used to bother her, but she was glad he still had the mischievous wink, the easy smile. "I'll just have the tomato juice with an omelet. Tell me what you're doing now that you're out of the service."

"I'm planning to sail around the world."

"What?"

"There's a big world out there. I want to see it."

"You've been reading too much Jack London or Joshua Slocum. Didn't you see enough in the Navy? For awhile anyway?" *Of course. He'll never settle for a traditional career.* One thing she loved about him was his daring to be different, his audacity.

"Only whetted my appetite. How about you?"

"I'll get a masters in psychology, maybe even a doctorate."

"Impressive. Hey, want to be my psychologist?" He laughed. "I'm sure you think I need one."

"Probably not. There's no hope for you anyway, is there? Actually, I'm not interested in clinical work except testing. I'd like to do research."

"So you won't psychoanalyze me."

"Promise! Besides, I like a little mystery."

After lunch they drove out in the country, less aware of the landscape than each other.

"Interesting we're here at the same time," Marty said. "I came home because Don Wagner died. What brought you back?"

"I came about two weeks ago to borrow money from my folks—a stake for my voyage. I read about the death in the paper."

He listened attentively while she described her family's connection to Don. But he expressed more interest in her Chicago life—prosaic as it seemed to her—compared to the adventures she imagined he had. She spiced up her life with tales about evenings on Rush Street, listening to Dixieland on the South Side, sailing with friends on Lake Michigan.

They stopped once to walk on the beach of a small, artificial lake—their summer swimming hole—now partially cleared of snow for skating. As they turned the corner of the bathhouse, Marty, exposed to the raw northwest wind, shivered until Wally put his arm around her waist, pulled her close. *Déjà vu. Just like my last afternoon with Rich.*

"Too cold? Want to go back to the car?"

"No. I want to watch that skater making the three-turns and waltz jumps. He's not bad." An undercurrent of excitement alarmed Marty but she stayed cradled in Wally's arm, prolonging this exhilarating moment, admiring the grace of the skater.

Back in the car, Wally faced her. "I've decided not to leave tomorrow. I want to spend more time with you."

Surprised, but pleased, Marty said, "Wally, I don't think you should change your plans on my account."

As he pulled up in front of her house, he asked, "Have dinner with me tonight?"

"I can't. I promised my parents I'd go to a movie with them."

"Tomorrow night, then?"

"I guess." She pulled away as he leaned toward her. "See you tomorrow." She leaped out of the car, hurried up the walk and waved as she entered her house. Inside, she picked up a letter from Rich and a baby shower invitation from Cathy that were sitting on the table near the front door, then rushed to the living room window to see him drive away.

After the Martin and Lewis movie, Marty reread Richard's letter, focusing on his comments about Don's death. He asked good questions without offering a new slant. But why should she expect him to solve the mystery when they failed? Later, she wrote to Rich:

> It's funny how one recovers from disaster. A week ago I was tied up in knots. I couldn't stretch out my legs or relax my fingers. I felt my heart was in my mouth and my stomach was so constricted I could hardly eat. Now I'm only tense

occasionally, mostly when Dad is distressed. If only the money would show up, we could move on.

My Chicago way of life is more important to me than I realized. Although I feel an integral part of this family, I no longer belong in this community. I'm a stranger, a sea polyp drifting until it finds an appropriate place to attach itself.

She put down her pen. *Is that place with Rich? The wife of a poor graduate student or university professor?* She met him in a humanities class and got to know him better in a genetics class. She refused a first date because she "had to wash her hair," but the week after she felt a twinge of excitement when he held her hand as they watched *King Solomon's Mines* at a theatre on 63rd Street. That spring when they worked on an anthropology project and an experiment on perfect pitch, she admired his intellect and his inventiveness. She loved the witty Valentine poem he wrote in fractured French, the trinkets—found objects—he gave her—especially the dime store ring presented on bended knee with his first marriage proposal and promise to bestow a diamond eventually.

Marty's hopes of returning to Chicago soared the next morning.

"I've decided to bid on Don's car," CB said, sitting down to breakfast. "We'll need two cars if we move. Your mother is a good walker, but Don's house is too far out."

"Good idea, Dad. Speaking of cars—any new information about the car parked on the side street near Don's garage?"

"Nothing new. The neighbor lady didn't know the make, only that it was gray and had four doors. The private detective's first job will be to locate that car. I'm also going to bid on Don's guns and his fishing tackle and Mrs. Wagner's diamond for your mother."

Good. Life may be returning to normal. Marty smiled.

By mid-afternoon Marty, tired of the piano and reading, annoyed at her restlessness, grabbed her coat and scarf and went for a walk. She wandered nowhere in particular, past her old grade school, past the East Side Grocery—where she bought penny candy as a child—toward the James River and away from town. She avoided unshoveled sidewalks, meandered like the river she approached, until the sun alerted her to the time, and she headed home.

When Wally picked her up, Marty noticed his car was gray. "Is this your Dad's car?"

"Yeah. He's been pretty decent about it. As long as I drop him off at work and pick him up. How about a drink at the Pheasant Lounge? We can eat there too. I hear they have great steaks."

One cocktail later, Marty was relaxed and talkative. "Wally, what did you do all week before I called you? There's so little to do here if you're not working or going to school." Before he could answer, their waitress appeared to take orders for a second drink.

They talked and laughed, both of them revealing bits of themselves in anecdotes, attempting to make up for the time they were out of touch. Twice young men approached who remembered Wally as a high school football hero. Both times Wally invited the young man to join them. Marty tried to be pleasant, but she resented the interruptions.

Later, over coffee, Wally said, "We need to go somewhere else so we can talk. I'd suggest my place, but my parents are there."

"Mine are home too," she laughed. "And they're expecting the Masons."

"Well, I'm sure we could find a motel."

Marty studied him. "Are you teasing or testing?"

"Suggesting."

"What if I said okay?"

"I'd say I know a place."

She hesitated. "I can't."

"Well, you said you hadn't changed." He put his hand on top of hers. "It's okay. You always were a bit prudish."

"Was I, really? As a true U of C student—and I don't mean Berkeley—I want your definition of prude."

"Would you accept prim and proper?"

"Accepted. But now I really should get home before the Mason's leave."

"I knew you'd revert to type! Marty, relax. It's only 9:30."

"It seems later. By the way, you didn't answer my question before. How do you keep busy all day? Did you date anyone before I called?"

"Jealous?"

"Of course not!"

"Now you've hurt my feelings."

"Seriously, Wally, with reading and practicing the piano—to say nothing of visiting my grandmother and trying to provide moral support for my parents—I still get bored."

"Marty, if you weren't here, I'd be gone by now. I've seen my parents and a couple of bankers. I've been reading and working out at the gym—a habit left over from school days." He started the car. "It's too early to go home. How about a nightcap at that little roadside tavern on the other side of the tracks?"

Marty agreed, but when they discovered the place was closed, they decided to call it a night. Despite the heater, both felt chilled in the cold and drafty car.

"Move over, Sweetie, it's freezing in here."

She shifted, but he pulled her even closer after he parked in front of her house. Snuggled next to him, Marty recalled evenings spent sitting on her stoop, fantasizing about their futures, until Ellen called from an upstairs window, reminding them of the time. *"Marty, it's getting late."* He talked about California so romantically, Marty finally accused him of naiveté, believing California was the be-all and end-all of life.

"Remember the night we went swimming in Lake Byron?" he asked.

She nodded. "I lost the class ring my Dad gave me. It's still hard to believe you found it in the sand in the dark." She also remembered that he ceremoniously slipped it on her finger and kissed the back of her hand. "Talk about luck."

"A night to remember."

"Yeah." Yet, soon after, she went east to school, angry, refusing to see him for a reason she could no longer remember, and he went west.

"I'd better go in before my mother sticks her head out the window. We've been parked here a long time. They'll think we froze to death or been asphyxiated."

"What would you like to do tomorrow?"

"Ice skate. But I accepted an invitation to a baby shower, so I'm not free 'til late in the day."

"I don't have skates and I probably couldn't stand up in them anyway. How about dinner again? A movie?"

"Okay, but I insist we go Dutch. You should be saving your money."

"Don't worry. I've got plenty. Pick you up at 7:00."

While Marty was writing her nightly letter to Richard, images of the evening with Wally kept intruding. Knowing Wally's departure was imminent, she considered inviting Rich to visit for a few days at the end of the quarter. She could introduce him to her hometown and he might convince CB to come to Chicago for a thorough physical. At the very least, she could return to Chicago with him.

The next morning Marty asked her mother, "Okay if I invite Richard for a short visit? No eggs for me. Just juice."

"A visit would be fine, Marty. CB?"

"Sure. I was starting to wonder if Wally had replaced him. One egg for me."

"We're just old friends." Marty sipped orange juice. "Did I tell you I'm going to Cathy's this afternoon?"

"Your mother tells me she has a baby."

"Yes, a girl, four or five months old." Great. Now he would be after her to produce a grandchild. "May I be excused?" She moved toward the piano. Others fled to the bathroom for privacy. She escaped to the piano, to Mozart, eventually Beethoven.

Cathy took Marty's coat and told her to join the group. Ruth, a former classmate approached. "Hi, Marty. Long time, no see. Have you seen Nancy's new diamond? She and Cliff are finally getting married—probably next fall."

"That's exciting. I'll look for her."

"Except for you, she's the last of the girls I knew well."

Marty approached two young women. Although she assumed the talk would be mostly about babies, she hoped her child development course would get her through. When the mother of a two-year-old told her she was beginning to toilet train her child, Marty started to say, "Dr. Spock . . ."

"Oh, Marty, I gave up on Spock long ago. He basically tells you to do whatever seems right to you."

"I guess I have a lot to learn." Marty retreated, wishing she could escape. When the gifts were opened. she thought of Gail and the drawers full of baby clothes. She wanted to feel the enthusiasm expressed by the other guests, but she didn't. *Why am I different? Am I lacking a gene?*

At the end of the party Marty declined a ride in order to walk home. She wanted to stop at the library, to revisit one of her favorite places. She loved to browse, to be surrounded by books—knowing she would never read more than a tiny fraction of a fraction of them, but also knowing she would never really be bored, because there would always be more to read. Walking up the steps, she stumbled toward the top. She cursed softly, annoyed at herself for forgetting about the taller step that tripped her as a kid until she stopped one day and figured it out.

Inside, the library had shrunk—like the church and the grade school. Marty walked toward the periodicals, wanting to appear purposeful, when the newspaper headline caught her eye. *STALIN DEAD*. She studied the photo. *Looks can be deceiving. His malevolence doesn't show on his face.* She wondered if Liz would count this as the second death. Surely, Grandma would be next, but could you count an evil Stalin with Don and Grandma?

Walking home, Marty decided Russians would not mourn Stalin like Americans mourned Roosevelt eight years earlier, despite Stalin's many more years in power. Who would be the new leader? She guessed a Stalin double would take over and nothing would change. Did anything change with Truman? *No one at the shower even mentioned Stalin's death!*

Wally was late. "I was supposed to pick my Dad up early on Saturday and I missed a couple of weeks ago. I thought we'd settled it, but he threw it up at me again. Sorry."

"If he wants the car tonight, we could walk."

"No, he doesn't want the car tonight and the Prairie Inn is too far for walking. It's across the river. Have you been there?" He rammed the stick shift into third.

"Hey, don't take it out on the car. No, but I've heard good reports about the new Prairie Inn restaurant. I understand the complex includes a bowling alley, a poolroom and a motel. Big deal for a little town."

"Well, I'm more than ready to leave this little 'burg. If it weren't for you, I'd be out of here and out of my parents' hair. And they'd be out of mine. I have the money. I'm flying to the coast on Saturday." He turned toward her. "Come with me."

"Ha," she laughed. "Why not? Give up everything I've worked toward?"

"You'd get a real education. You wouldn't regret it."

"Maybe not today or tomorrow . . . Oh my God, I'm quoting Humphrey Bogart! *Casablanca*! Guess what. You'd regret it even before I did!"

"Not unless you got washed overboard!"

"Oh, stop."

They crossed the James River, heading away from town on a main road, passed under a railroad trestle, past the ruins of a small brewery that burned to the ground long before her time. "I wonder why some people get attached to places and others don't. Why do I love this place, why do I love the prairie—while you can hardly wait to get away?"

"How could anyone get attached to this town? Or the prairie? It's so boring—nothing but empty space."

"No buildings, no cars, you can see to the horizon and the sky is close. I love it. Have you ever heard a Western meadowlark?"

"Probably. Here we are."

Marty shifted her attention to this new addition to the town. They entered a large dining room, attractive with white tablecloths and candles, a stone fireplace, a few prairie relics—including a collection of Indian arrowheads. Seated at a small table near a window, Marty could see the motel entrance—a multi-colored neon sign flashing over the door.

"Marty, did you ever do anything spontaneously? Anything unplanned?"

"Maybe not, so what? I admit I'm practical. Maybe that's my tragic flaw. But what will you do when your money runs out?"

"I have enough for a long time. Why worry about it until it happens?"

"Some of us are worriers I guess. I blame it on growing up during the Depression, then the war, and now the bomb. But you grew up then too."

"And we had no control over any of those things. Why not take what pleasures you can whenever you can? Why not have fun? Live it up while you can? We've already had another war."

"I *am* having fun in Chicago, living it up in a different way. I like student life. I'll graduate and get a job I really like. And what will you be doing?"

"I'll be doing what I like—seeing the world. I can get a job anytime. I don't mind physical labor. And, anyway, I have almost $10,000 enough for a long time." He turned toward the waiter.

"You borrowed all of that from your parents?"

"Marty, how do you want your steak?"

"Medium rare."

"Remember the time we were home from college," he said after the waiter left, "and we broiled steak on the ancient stove in your parents' lake cottage."

"How could I forget? We destroyed a lot of good meat."

"I'll never forget you in those pink shorts running on the beach."

"But wasn't that the summer you joined the Navy?" *That's how it ended. I knew I couldn't wait four years.*

"It was going to be the Army or the Navy." Before coffee arrived, Wally resurrected the earlier discussion. "Marty, it's a cliché, but we're only young once. I don't think my proposed adventure is irresponsible. 'Don't put off until tomorrow' makes sense to me." He laughed. "One cliché deserves another. Would you like a liqueur?"

"Yes, thanks. I guess it's not irresponsible if you can afford it, but I'm amazed anyone would give you money to do it."

"What flavor?"

"Oh, coffee or orange." Suddenly, she couldn't face him. He had a large sum of money from an unknown source, he drove a gray four-door sedan, and a couple of Saturdays ago, he was late picking up his father from work. It was crazy, absurd. *Wally would never . . .*

"Hey, come back here. What are you brooding about now?"

"Don's death," she said, trying to face him squarely.

"I'm sorry, Marty. I guess you were pretty close to him. Ah, our drinks are here just in the nick of time. Let me tell you more about the trip."

As they sipped their drinks, he talked about New Zealand and Australia, islands in the South Pacific reminiscent of the war, India and Africa. The idea of Greece and the Greek Islands captivated her the most—Athens, Sparta, the Peloponnese, the Aegean—the cradle of Western Civilization.

"Fabulous! I'd love to hear more," Marty said, her admiration rekindled by his enthusiasm and ingenuity. Transported briefly to an imagined classical world, she failed to notice they were the last people in the restaurant.

"We'd better leave before they sweep us out," Wally said. As they stood near the door, he helped her with her coat. "Should we stay here?"

"Sure. We can talk some more."

"Talk," he repeated. "Okay. I'll get us a room."

Trudging through the snow, looking for number 127, Marty put her arm through his, confident no one she knew saw her heading for a motel room. *I'm as bad as my mother, worrying about the neighbors.* "One twenty-seven is my lucky number," she said. "My locker number."

"You remember the number?"

"I had the same locker for three years. Yours must have been 129."

"Sounds right." Wally opened the door and stepped aside. She turned on the light to find a pleasant, if modest, room—not shabby as she half-expected. When he touched her shoulder, she started.

"Relax. Let me have your coat." Before he hung their coats in a small closet, he took a bottle from his pocket. He found glasses in the bathroom.

"It's freezing in here." Marty looked for a way to turn the heat up.

"I've got it. The controls are in here." He emerged from the bathroom. "This will help 'til the heat comes up. I hope you like Scotch and water. I guess we won't miss the ice. Pretend you're English."

"I really don't need anything, but maybe it will warm me up." She sat on a straight back chair as she tasted it. He sat on the bed facing her.

"You need this more than I do," he said, slipping off a beige, cashmere sweater and standing up to slip it over her head.

"Thanks. It's a bit big. Help me roll up the sleeves." He knelt in front of her, laughing as he worked on one sleeve, then the other. Before he got up, he leaned forward to kiss her. She did not resist, did not want to resist. When he finally broke away and pulled her toward him and the bed, she pushed back.

"You promised," she said. "We were talking about Greece. Tell me more."

"All right. Sit next to me so my sweater can keep us both warm." He propped two pillows against the headboard and she curled up next to him as he began to paint verbally vivid land and seascapes of the Greek Islands and Mediterranean seaports, the Riviera and the Costa del Sol.

"You need a small fortune to take such a fantasy trip. I didn't think your parents had that kind of money."

"They don't."

"You've got a rich friend?" She was feeling the alcohol. He didn't answer. When he sat on the bed again, he kissed her and she returned it. They had one more day. "Why are you leaving so soon? We may never see each other again."

"I didn't think you cared. I have to be in San Francisco on Sunday. When I made those plans, I had no idea you'd show up. What's so funny?" He smiled, amused, as she started to giggle.

"I have another cliché: Make hay while the sun shines. Only the sun isn't shining. My luck."

"I'd never let that stop me." He kissed her again. Marty let her feeling take over until he got up for another drink. She sat on the edge of the bed.

"Rich . . . I mean Wally. It's very late. I've got to go home."

Sneaking in the front door never worked for Marty. Ellen, a light sleeper, always let both daughters know she heard them come in. Beyond that she said little. But they knew she knew and their guilt kept them in line. Marty, too tired now to think, was grateful she could put off facing her parents and the dissonance in her head.

Chapter Eleven

Soggy Letters

Letters were arriving regularly now, but Richard received no signs Marty would return soon. Half-heartedly, he worked on applications to graduate schools and the required autobiography that forced him to consider his future. If he left Chicago, would Marty join him? Would she marry him? They both liked Chicago, thought no other school compared, but they'd never been anywhere else. Maybe she wouldn't leave.

Several friends invited Richard to dinner, but Gail's invitations were most welcome. One evening they discussed Marty's inheritance and how they would spend the money if it were theirs. While Gail and Bill opted for a car, furniture, and clothing, Richard fantasized a year in Mexico—a complete break from school.

"You and Marty could do that, since you're only responsible for yourselves," Gail said, rubbing her belly. "But what would you do there?"

"Explore Mayan ruins and drink tequila? Ever since the anthropology course with Redfield, Yucatan has attracted me. And Marty took a Spanish course once."

On his way home, Richard detoured to Marty's apartment. He sat at her kitchen table wishing his hand could record as fast as his brain generated thoughts. First, he reported Bill's concern about her father's uncontrolled diabetes. Next, a bit apologetically, he tackled ideas for spending her inheritance.

Above all, Marty you should invest in yourself—possibly by going to school full time. No outside job for at least a year. I'm still hoping you will come with me to graduate school—whichever one it is. Living in Mexico for a year would be more fun (I think), but I'm not sure you would be willing to leave school right now for an indolent life style. Of course, you might tap into a creative vein—write poetry like Amy Lowell or Emily Dickinson. I think you're flexible enough to make a good life out of any life. And as much as I look forward to talking with you about this, you must decide for yourself. I feel certain you won't buy clothing and a car in the style of Bill and Gail. Strange, isn't it, such close friends valuing different things.

My eyes are burning out of my head because I'm not getting enough sleep. I should go to bed. Honey, letters are such poor substitutes for you. And writing is a poor way to express how much I love you. If only I could hug you just once. I miss you so much, I forget how things are with you. It's amazing how emotions skew perceptions and conceptions so that what looks like an absolute in one situation looks like trivia in another.

My doldrums will disappear
When once again my honey's near.

It's her I miss
I want her kiss.
      See how tired I am ?
      With absolute love,

    Rich

Although he worried about writing so much he would antagonize Marty, his fears dissipated when her invitation to South Dakota arrived two days later. He could leave in two weeks when the quarter ended, if he finished his work and found someone to assume his lab responsibilities. Days might drag more than ever now, but an end was in sight. He returned to the lab that afternoon with renewed energy and walked to Marty's apartment in the evening, planning to study.

When he opened the door, he found a half-inch of water on the kitchen floor. Looking for the janitor, he found Ed mopping up his floors next door.

"What the hell happened here?"

"The radiators leaked. I think the janitor forgot to close a valve or something. Something to do with the boiler. It's fixed now. Except the mess."

Richard, relieved only the kitchen was flooded, started to mop up. When he noticed damp lines in the ceiling plaster, he checked the other two rooms and discovered the same problem. He also found cardboard cartons in a closet off the kitchen, saturated from sitting on the wet floor. Two were filled with papers that he carefully removed and spread out on the living room floor. Besides term papers and class notes, he found several letters at the bottom of one box.

He hesitated, not sure how to handle the letters, afraid Marty might be offended if she thought he read her mail. On the other hand, she might be annoyed if he did not try to save it. He found a towel to soak up what he could, then gently slipped the letters out of their envelopes, carefully separating the pages, and laying them on the old carpet. All were signed "Wally" and postmarked Berkeley, California.

Uncertain about what to do next, he sat staring at the sea of paper around him. He tried to rationalize curiosity, knowing it would prevail over guilt. He checked dates first, thinking he might read only the most recent and discovered they covered a period of about two years. To his relief, none were recent—nothing dated during his time with Marty.

Picking up the letter closest to him, Richard began to read. He skimmed paragraphs about Berkeley, concentrating on the personal.

> Wished you were here yesterday—and all the days, for that matter, Bright Eyes. Went sailing with friends—swam off the boat and partied. Then returned to the frat house for food and more partying. Great time. Perfect day, except you weren't here. When are you going to drop those dry Greek philosophers and come have some fun? How about spring break? You do get a spring break at Chicago ?
>
> Stay alert, I sent you a gift!
> Love You, Gorgeous
> Wally

Amused one minute, angry the next, Richard had to acknowledge the amorous, juvenile comments were hardly more stupid than his own. He wondered how Marty responded. As they became repetitive, he began to lose interest in the letters but not the letter writer. He found Marty's picture album and looked for the football player, flanked by cheerleaders. He studied the snapshot briefly, closed up the apartment, and left in the direction of Gail's. She must know about this guy.

Outside in the cold, crisp air, Richard remembered his invitation to South Dakota and tried to dismiss the letters. The most recent was almost four years old. Still, could he ask Gail about Wally without seeming ridiculous?

Gail opened the door a crack and peeked around it.

"Okay to come in for ten minutes?"

"Of course, Rich. Coffee? There might be a beer in the fridge."

"Coffee's fine. Thanks. Where's Bill?"

Gail poured a cup of coffee. "He's in the shower. He's leaving for the hospital soon. What's up, Rich? You never come over this late."

Richard described the wet mess in Marty's apartment, his dilemma with the damp mail. "I think I saved most of it."

"I'm sure you did the best you could."

"Most of them were from Wally."

"Oh, love letters."

Richard felt nauseous looking at the black coffee. "Do you have any milk? Gail, did you know him?"

"Yes and no. I'll get the milk. I never met him. He was a student at Berkeley."

"How did you know about him?"

"Marty got a midnight phone call. We were roommates in the dorm. She had to explain why she got called to the househead's apartment in the middle of the night. They exchanged letters after that. It was a long time ago, about the time she started dating Carl."

"If she was seeing Carl, why was she writing to this other character?"

"Rich, you'll have to ask her. Wally was an old high school friend. That's all I know. Marty and I never talked much about him or men in general for that matter."

"I thought women did."

"Some do, but not Marty. Before Bill, I talked to an older sister. If Marty doesn't confide in you, maybe she talks to Liz. I doubt it, though."

"I guess we both know her that well." Richard looked up as Bill came in. "Hi! I just came over to pester your wife."

"Rich, I need to leave. Are you coming?" He kissed Gail. "See you in the morning, Sweetheart."

Opening the door to the street, Bill said, "Surprised to see you so late."

Richard told him about the water at Marty's without mentioning the letters. "I forgot to tell Gail, I have an invitation to South Dakota."

"I'll tell her. Leaving at the end of the quarter?"

"Yeah, not sure what day. Bill, what's your secret? I can't convince Marty to marry me. Any suggestions?"

"No. She'll come around. This is where we part. See ya later."

Gail's comment about Marty's confiding in him troubled him. He never talked to Marty about his old flames, but he'd never saved old letters either. When he got to his apartment, he read all the letters from her, gratified by how frequently she professed her love, but mindful of how undemonstrative she was in general. The invitation to South Dakota must mean something. How long would she save his letters?

Turning on the radio and tuning in WFMT, he hoped classical music would soothe his ruffled ego as he began his next letter to Marty. Writing about the mess in the apartment was easy enough. He admitted to spreading out wet papers and mail, but gave no clue he had done more. He told her he might hitch a ride to SD, weather permitting, or take the Dakota 400, since he could not find a car to deliver—his usual transportation when he went east. He ended:

> This separation is terrible—and at least ten more days of it. I'll write a longer letter tomorrow and call you on the pipe.

> I love you, Bushel and a Peck
> Rich

For a moment he considered asking a question about Wally, hoping it would be less revealing of his feelings, more matter-of-fact, than a face to face question. In the end he decided to wait.

Chapter Twelve

Exit Wally

When Marty awoke the next morning, she lay quietly watching the dust particles dance in the sunlight streaming in the east window. She stretched, loving the flexibility of her body. If only her head would stop pounding. Should she tell her father about Wally's money and his gray car? She didn't believe Wally was guilty of anything. But what if he was and she let him slip away? And Rich?

Aspirin and a shower dulled her headache. By the time she appeared in the kitchen, she almost felt ready to face her mother. Ellen had cleared the table, excepting dishes and silverware for Marty.

"Dad gone already?" Marty asked, knowing he would be. Still, she missed his *Good morning, Mary Sunshine.*

"Already? It's almost noon." Ellen paused briefly, "You came in very late."

"I know. I'm sorry, Mom." She doubted she would ever feel like an adult in her parent's home.

"What can you find to do at that hour?"

"Mostly talk. We haven't seen each other in years."

"Scrambled eggs?" Ellen asked.

"Yes, thanks." Marty poured herself a cup of coffee and put bread in the toaster. She'd try to eat despite her unsettled stomach.

"You know I don't approve of your behavior, but you're too old to scold and it wouldn't do any good anyway."

"Thanks, Mom. Any new developments? Don has been dead for two weeks and there's still unanswered questions."

"We go over the same thing every night. Nothing new, not even from the detective."

"Mom, do you think the money is in the house?"

"No, but I do hope your Dad decides we should move there."

Sitting at the piano, trusting her fingers to take over, Marty concentrated on her dilemma. Although she doubted Wally could be guilty of a serious crime, the coincidences frightened her. Should she share this with her father—so emotionally involved, so desperate for resolution? If only she knew where Wally got the money for his adventure. And what should she tell Rich? Soon, inattention compromised her playing; her fingers needed more input from her head. She tried to stay focused on the music, but her mind kept drifting, her fingers faltering. She was grateful when the phone rang.

"You'll never guess what I found in the basement," Wally said.

"A frog, a dead mouse? I give up."

"Ice skates that fit. If you really want to skate, I'm willing to try. You may have to hold me up."

"I'd love to. How soon?"

"Half hour."

Marty was looking for warm socks when Wally arrived, so Ellen answered the door. Before she got downstairs, Marty heard their laughter. *He hasn't lost his touch with women, his charm and knack for flattery.* His knowing smile and wink as she walked into the room did not surprise her, or his insistence on carrying her skates to the car. After he put the skate bag on the back seat, he leaned forward to kiss her, but she put up her hand to stop him. "Not now. Mom is probably watching out the window."

"She likes me," he answered. "She has good taste."

"She likes all my boyfriends." Marty smiled at him. "Drive straight down Idaho Avenue. I'll tell you when to stop." As he drove, she told him the city used to flood this vacant lot during the years she was in grade school. "Oh no! This is it. Where the bungalow is."

"Sure you've got the exact location?"

"Yes, Anna Otis and I skated here after school—fourth, fifth, sixth grades. We'd chase the boys and play crack the whip."

"You chased the boys? I should have known you in those days. Where to now?"

"Damn. I guess we'll have to go the lake. Where we saw the skater the other day." As they drove down Third Street toward the river, Marty wrestled with questions. *Why hasn't he mentioned last night? Should I tell him about Rich? How can I approach the money question? Obviously, he knows money is missing, so why doesn't he tell me who gave him such a large sum?*

Wally finally broke the silence when he pulled into a parking space. "You're very quiet. I'd give at least a penny for your thoughts."

"I'm confused," she said honestly. "I don't know what to say."

"About what?" he hesitated. "Last night? I enjoyed it. But it ended too soon."

"Oh, let's get on the ice." She wanted desperately to skate away from her thoughts. She laced her skates quickly and put on the guards.

On the ice her mood lightened. Within minutes she felt secure. "It's like riding a bike or getting your sea legs," she said, skating around Wally, "not that I know much about sea legs."

"I hope you're right," Wally struggled to stay upright. Eventually, they raced and Marty taught him what she could remember about edges and simple figures. "How do you know all this?" he asked, a willing but clumsy learner.

"A friend in college had some coaching." Both were exhausted when they decided to quit. Marty's toes were white when she took her skates and socks off in the car.

"Your toes look frostbitten." Wally took off his gloves. "Here, slip your feet into these. They're warmer than your socks or anything in the car. I'll get the heater going."

"It was stupid to stay out there so long, but it was fun. Don't worry about my toes. They'll be okay. I'll put them near the heater. Reminds me of my childhood when we'd skate until dark no matter how cold it was."

"We're close to the Prairie Inn. Let's get warm there while we have a drink."

Wally sat next to her in a booth near the fireplace and ordered two hot buttered rums.

"What a great time and we didn't break our necks," Marty said, energized by the exercise. But as she absorbed the alcohol and the nicotine and smoke from cigarettes, her energy waned. She resisted an urge to curl up next to Wally. The money issue began to resound in her head like the dominant chord in one of her piano pieces. Thoughts of Richard also surfaced, a minor theme.

"Smell that food, Marty. Let's have dinner here again. The food last night was okay. What do you say? I'm starving."

"I'm hungry too. But I'd better call home. Let them know I won't be there."

She found a phone booth next to the door. Ellen answered on the second ring. "Marty, why don't you bring Wally here for dinner. Your Dad and I would love to see him."

"Thanks Mom, we kind of want to be alone. It's his last night. You know he leaves tomorrow."

"All right, then. Say goodbye to him for me."

"Okay, Mom." Walking back to their table, Marty decided to stay focused on Wally's journey. After he ordered the steak dinners and wine, she said, "Tell me more about your trip."

"I'll be sailing out of San Francisco without an itinerary, so I can only speculate on destinations," he said. "I'll decide which ports I want to explore once I get there."

"I can't imagine going on a long trip—even a short one—without a plan," she said. "How do you know how much money you'll need?"

"I don't, exactly. Oh, here's our wine." The waiter poured a small amount of wine into one of the glasses and waited for Wally to taste it. He winked at Marty as he sniffed the wine. "You should probably do this. I'm better at Scotch."

Momentarily, Marty was more interested in the waiter who reminded her of a boy she fancied in the eighth grade. "Are you a Fitzgerald by any chance?" she asked.

"No," he answered, "but I have Fitzgerald cousins."

"Eddie and Patrick?"

"Yeah. How'd you know?"

"Lucky guess." After he left, she added, "Small town and strong family resemblance. I had a crush on Eddie years ago."

"Frankly, I'm more interested in your current crushes."

"Oh, I don't have crushes any more." She welcomed the waiter's return this time with food, a priority over curiosity for both. But as she ate, she began to wonder what Richard would think about her attempt to discover the source of Wally's money. How hurt and angry would he be if he knew about last night? Would he walk out of her life? This might be a test of his love for her, but he might see it as a test of her love for him. Marty sighed.

"Everything okay?" Wally asked. "You seem preoccupied. Why the heavy sigh?"

"Just dreaming about your potential adventures." To avoid his gaze, she spread butter on a roll, thinking how adept she'd become at dissimulating.

"You know, I really can't see you on a tramp steamer, even though I'd love to take you along."

"Hey, I have a steamer trunk," she smiled. "If I had the guts, I'd be well equipped. I guess I'd need money too."

"Not if you're willing to sell your body." He winked again. "You're a handsome wench. You'd be well paid. But you're about to inherit money, so you don't need to do anything so drastic."

"I don't have money yet. Probate Court can take several months—even longer."

"You could get a bank loan."

"I'll think about it." Marty sipped her wine. "Is that what you did? Get a bank loan?"

"Not exactly. Are we staying?" Wally asked as the waiter cleared away their dinner plates.

"Yes. I want to hear more."

Before they left the restaurant, Wally bought another bottle of wine and got a room key. Outside, he headed for his car to get the bottle of Scotch he stashed earlier. Marty stood, relishing the cold, crisp air and the fresh, white snow swirling around them. "I love winter when it's like this." She paused. "I see you still like Chivas Regal."

"Yes, the wine is for you—unless you'd like Scotch."

"I don't think either of us needs anything," she answered. *Would another drink open him up?* She was beginning to feel like a failed spy. Briefly, she stood frozen, trying to weigh the value of any information she might discover. *Why don't I just give up? Don is dead. Nothing will change that.*

"Hey, what's the matter?"

"Nothing. Turned my ankle." She lied again, amazed at her deviousness. *No turning back now.*

Inside, Wally mixed his drink and poured a glass of wine for Marty. "If you change your mind and decide you'd prefer a real drink to this rot-gut wine, let me know." He sat on the bed, put his feet up. "Tell me more about your life in Chicago. I haven't heard much about your work or your friends."

"I'm sure you'll find it dull. I've been testing adolescents for a big research project."

"What are you finding out?"

"We've just begun to score and analyze test data. We won't have results for a long time."

"How about boyfriends? How about Rich? You mentioned him last night."

So he heard. "I know I don't have as many as you have girlfriends."

As he got up to mix another drink, Wally said, "That's hardly an answer. Who's Rich?"

"A lab partner I had in an experimental psych course. Wally, I have an idea. If I decided to go with you, could I get a loan from your benefactor? I'd pay it back with interest as soon as I could."

"Sweetie, you'd never go on a trip like this."

"And you don't really want me to." She slumped back on the bed, hoping he'd deny it.

"Only because I think you'd be unhappy. I told you, I have no goals, no plans, no specific expectations. I'm restless. I need to keep moving—for now, anyway. You have aspirations, goals. If you don't pursue them, you'll be miserable and hate me in the long run."

"I'd be wretched."

"What?"

"Wretched. A word I picked up from Tolstoy." She laughed without humor. Before she saw it coming, he put his arms around her and bent down to kiss her. The only thing left was to ask him directly. Could she do that? She returned his kiss. Maybe she'd feel emboldened after they made love.

Sitting next to Wally as he drove her home, Marty knew this was her last chance. She took a deep breath, closed her eyes, "Wally, who gave you the money?"

"My Uncle Ben. He always liked me. I should have gone to him in the first place."

Marty hated goodbyes. Usually they were temporary, so she could be casual, light-hearted. This was different. When they kissed at the door, she could not let go, clutched by the certainty she would never see him again, a fear she voiced, hoping to ward off the certainty of it happening—a superstition she no longer denied. He said nothing, only kissed her again.

As she entered the house, her future seemed as obscure as the dark hallway. She fumbled for the light switch, already nostalgic for a future that could never happen.

Tactile memories washed over Marty as she awoke the next morning. She felt good—happy her suspicions were unfounded—as she relived the last couple of days. She got up when she heard her father leave and went downstairs.

"There's a letter from Richard. I put it next to your plate."

"Thanks, Mom." Marty poured herself a cup of coffee and put a slice of bread in the toaster. "No eggs today." She opened the letter while she sipped coffee and waited for the toaster. "Rich says I should spend the money on education or—you'll love this—a year in Mexico being creative." *Going to Mexico sounds like Wally; being creative sounds like Rich.*

"What does he mean 'being creative?'"

"Writing poetry, I guess." To atone for coming in so late, she continued to read to Ellen about Bill's take on CB's health. When she came to the poem, she put the letter down and buttered her toast. Even if Richard weren't terribly corny, she could not share this personal stuff. She ate her toast and left the kitchen while Ellen worked on a casserole for dinner.

As Marty read Richard's silly poem, the horror of her betrayal began to resonate through her head and heart, a crescendo of guilt and fear that she had destroyed her relationship with Richard. Could she convince him she made a terrible mistake, that she truly loved only him? Was there any way she could undo what she had done?

Chapter Thirteen

Marty's Regrets

When Richard wrote about the flooded apartment, Marty remembered the old letters from Wally. If Rich read them, she knew he'd ask questions. What if she told him first? She sat at the piano, once again on automatic pilot, her fingers wandering over the keys while she speculated about her future with Richard. Her eagerness to see him overrode her concern about how things would turn out.

Everyday she wrote him long letters about visits to her grandmother, her father's vacillation about moving into Don's house, his health and her increasing restlessness.

> Dad's frequent choking spells scare me. He also has periods when he seems totally preoccupied, withdrawn. I guess his insistence on inviting the Masons, Jessie or other company over every night is good.
>
> You know how much I admire him for his strong beliefs and loyalties (though I disagree with

the Republicanism), but I am embarrassed by his public name-calling. Last night at the city commissioners meeting he disagreed with the mayor on an economic issue and called him a "stinker." Still, I identify more with him than Mom. Behind his stern exterior, I think he is just as sensitive as she is. He's more principled in some ways. Keeping up with the Jones is unimportant to him. I'm convinced Mom's early life of poverty and hard work toughened her to loss and deprivation in some ways, but also made her needier. Is that contradictory?

How lucky I have been. Although I lived through the Depression and WWII, I never felt deprived, never suffered any major losses. Even now, I will remember Don fondly, but my life will go on. And unless you're holding out on me, you've not suffered any major losses either. The service provided you with a trip to the Far East and an inexpensive education—to date, anyway!

As the days passed, Marty played over and over in her head her behavior with Wally. Could Richard ever trust her again? What if she had slept with Wally before she met Rich? She did not hold him accountable for love affairs before they met. But if he behaved now as she had, she'd be devastated. On the other hand, she'd never expect Wally to be faithful.

Looking for reassurance, Marty reread the most hopeful ending to one of Richard's letters: "I love you today, tonight, tomorrow and tomorrow. And forever—and no matter what— or why." His words warmed her heart, but they also kindled guilt. Did she love him less than he loved her?

Often she turned to her parents' argument for respite from her own conflict, usually siding with her father.

"CB, you must decide about moving," Ellen repeated nightly.

"Mom, how can you expect Dad to be comfortable in that house, to sleep there?"

"We won't be sleeping in Don's bedroom."

Her mother's response irritated Marty, but she let it drop. *That will be my room when I visit.*

Later that night Marty wrote to Richard:

> I'm getting tired of my self-pitying and mismatched parents. I'm so glad you and I have basically the same values. Our problems will be resolvable. I wish Mother could be a little more philosophical. I don't think she understands how Dad feels.

The next day Marty did not receive a letter from Richard. Disappointed, her frustration, exacerbated by her parents' constant bickering and her sense of failure and guilt, like a festering infection, came to a head and erupted into a terse, harsh note:

> Richard, I am so angry at you for not writing more and, especially, for not returning the only newspaper clippings of Don's death my parents had. Why did you send them to your parents? Please get them back to us as soon as possible. Maybe we can't resolve our problems either.

No sooner had she mailed the note than she regretted it and wrote again:

> Rich, please ignore that last letter. I'm sorry about all the bitching I've done. Maybe I'm getting worse than my mother. I'm at a loss to know how to deal with my parents—the disagreement about Don's house and especially Dad's vacillation.

And I know it takes a long time to write even a short letter—it's just that it takes such a short time to read even a long letter.

Please come by train—soon. I miss you. I love you. I can hardly wait for you to get here.

All my love,
Marty

Two days later CB announced at dinner. "We probably should move soon to avoid vandalism. The police chief told me some kids were hanging out behind Don's garage last night."

"Vandalism never occurred to me. Any damage?" Marty asked.

"Apparently not. I'd also like more time to search the house."

"After all the looking?"

"The money has to be somewhere. There must be a nook or cranny we missed. A drawer, under the mantel clock, even tucked into a book."

"I suppose." If her father really believed the money was there, he had to accept death as suicide. Easier to accept than murder because Don willed it? Ellen said little at dinner. *She knows she's going to get her way, finally.*

After dinner, Ellen asked Marty to look at *House Beautiful* magazines with her. "We'll have to paint several rooms before we move in. I could use some advice."

"It's settled then?" Marty expected more resistance from her father.

"I think so. I guess your father believes it's what Don wanted, so he wants it."

And it's the only way to achieve peace in the family. Would it become a weapon for him? Although she had no interest in home decorating, Marty sat with Ellen looking at pages of fancy kitchens and living rooms. She jumped up quickly when the phone rang.

"Marty, how could you write such a vicious letter?"

"Rich, I'm so sorry. Did you get my apology?"

"No."

"You'll get a written apology. Actually, I was going to call you the next time I was home alone."

"I just don't see how you could be so angry. I'll get the clippings back to you real soon. Sending them to my parents was so much easier than trying to write about it."

"I know you'll get them back. I'm sorry. Are you coming soon?"

"Wednesday, I think."

"It will be so good to see you. It's definitely time for me to get out of here."

"Finally! I hate your sister for leaving it all up to you. God, I miss you. It gets worse and worse. I get your hostile letter one day and then nothing the next."

"I forget to send airmail sometimes. You're coming by train?"

"Probably, I can't find a car to deliver and hitchhiking seems risky this time of year. I don't want to get stranded on the prairie."

"Good. Definitely don't hitchhike." Marty made sure her parents were out of earshot and continued *sotto voce*. "It looks as if the folks will move into Don's house early next month. Dad's concerned about vandalism now. And he still thinks they might find the money."

"What do you think?"

"I hope the bickering ends. At least the process of moving will keep them occupied. How are Gale and Bill and Spence and Ed? I miss them all."

"Ed stops over. So do George and Dave. Gail feeds me occasionally. I've been busy, but it's your letters that keep me going. Your apartment is okay—no problems since the flood. All your instructors have been accommodating and I've sent the graduate school applications except Chicago and Michigan's. By the way, should I bring anything from your apartment?"

"I guess not. Not even the little gadget in the medicine cabinet. We won't be sleeping in the same bedroom. I'm sure you guessed that. And my mother is a very light sleeper."

"Okay. Let me know if there's something you want. And do me a favor. Never write another letter like that."

"Richie, please believe me. That letter was a horrible mistake."

"I wish you could promise we'd never be separated again."

"I certainly hope we won't be. Rich, we'd better end this conversation. My folks will think you're a spendthrift, making an unnecessary call."

"Bye kiddo. See ya soon. I love you, Bushel and a Peck."

After the phone call, Marty began her next letter to Richard. She apologized again and then reported on the latest visit to her grandmother. Tears welled up as she wrote:

> Grandma was half-aware something was wrong. She cried and kept asking how it all started, then she would scold because she didn't have her clothes or anything to do. Mother said she was like that right after the stroke, but I had not seen it before. It reminded me how busy she'd always been—making hooked rugs, crocheted tablecloths, linens decorated with cross-stitching, painting china (long before I was born; she painted the large blue and gold set in our china closet).
>
> As we were about to leave, she said, "The children are coming." It seemed strange because she doesn't recognize my father. I also remembered that when I was growing up, she often mentioned her children but never her husband. Maybe because he'd been dead so many years. I don't know if my sadness arises from her approaching death or recognizing the fragility of human capacity. The woman I knew is dead, and I'm grieving for a woman I loved but hardly knew, since she lived most of her life before I was born.

I try to convince myself that dwelling on the aged, incoherent creature inhabiting my grandmother's shriveled shell, the grandmother whose mental circuits were destroyed almost as completely as an electrical circuit blown out by lightening, is pointless. I try to think of her life as not easy in the early years, but not tragic or wasted. At times I feel angry that she has to die this way. I'm not sure I really understand it, but Donne captures something in . . . *any man's death diminishes me.*

See you soon. I love you,
Marty

Giving in to her laziness the next day, Marty stretched out on the sofa, appreciating the solitude and her parents' acceptance of her not attending church with them. She wondered about her father's transformation. He told her once that he intended to join the Methodist Church, but skipped out when his young friends began declaring their belief and faith in God. He didn't want to stoop to their level of hypocrisy. Did he believe now? He could have used the snow that fell during the night as an excuse to stay home and shovel.

With her hand Marty traced the carved frame at the back of the brown horsehair sofa, the silent witness to childhood games and adolescent necking. How often had she lain here with a sore throat or childhood illness, transfixed by the apparent motion of the circular medallion around the overhead light fixture, waiting for Ellen to read her a story or take her temperature? Suddenly, Wally dominated her thoughts. *Forget him. I doubt I could be happy with him even if he were available.* She reached for the *Minneapolis Star*, determined to put him out of mind.

When her parents arrived home with Jessie, Marty put down the funnies and joined them in the kitchen. Although she no longer expected a revelation, she listened for hints. It seemed uncharacteristic of Jessie to conceal information, but maybe a spinster of her generation could not acknowledge a generous gift from a man. If she had a secret, Jessie kept it as they discussed the sermon they heard that morning.

After lunch, Marty volunteered to go with CB to see his mother. She knew she'd be devastated if it were Ellen who was dying. And she doubted CB really believed his mother was improving. Her agitation, her crying and scolding, did not change. *What is she reliving?* Marty felt helpless, holding the aged hand.

Chapter Fourteen

Tying up Loose Ends

Richard reread the disturbing letter from Marty. Although she apologized profusely on the phone, he did not see how boredom and restlessness—or her parent's bickering—could trigger such a vitriolic attack. Her words stung.

He wrote to his parents reminding them to return the clippings, and he began another letter to Marty trying to work through his confusion and pain:

> Marty, I worry that you don't love me—or love me enough. I know I'm neurotic when it comes to you. I channel all my worry, all my dysphoria, into my feelings about you and our relationship. My fear is that you will stop loving me because you only respect strong-willed people who concentrate on achievement. Sometimes I feel like kicking myself for not having more pride and purpose. I feel like I'm weak (like Fitzgerald)

instead of strong (like Hemingway or Faulkner). I just can't be tough when it comes to you.

Although he started writing with the intention of being honest, he sensed his self-abasement verging on dishonesty. He shifted to his latest contact with Gail and Bill, hoping to neutralize any negative reactions to what he wrote about himself. He ended:

Please don't write another letter like that ever again. And maybe you should stop reading Russian literature, since the Russians overreact and get emotional at such damnable things.

He mailed the letter on the way to work the next morning. *Not many more letters to write, and only one more weekend to get through—if all goes as scheduled.* He and Seth should finish collecting flicker fusion data on Monday and his last exam was on Tuesday. Depending on the train schedule, he could leave Wednesday or Thursday. He'd ask Spence to look after the lab animals and Ed to keep an eye on Marty's apartment.

Approaching the Midway, he took the road that bisected the veterans' housing area. Surrounded by the gray, pre-fabricated units, he speculated on which drab-fab he and Marty would inherit if she married him and they stayed in Chicago. Not that it mattered, since all the units were the same. The dregs of grimy snow, leafless trees and shrubs and the metallic colored March sky made a dismal, uninviting setting, but budding trees, flowering shrubs and greening lawns would camouflage the ugliness in a few weeks.

Crossing the Midway, he entered the quadrangle through the archway between Classics and Harper. He passed Blake-Gates and Cobb Hall, turned left toward Ellis Avenue and the bookstore. Unsure of the time, he hurried past the University Press and dashed up the steps of the Psychology Department, an old apartment building that housed faculty offices, a library and a shop in the basement where equipment for experiments was made. He stuck his head into the first floor front office. "Hi, Alice. Seth in yet?"

"He called to say he'd be late. You're supposed to go ahead and set up."

"Thanks. You know, we all think of you as the 3-in-1 oil that keeps the department running smoothly."

"Tell the chairman. Maybe he'll raise my pay!"

When Seth arrived, he motioned Richard into his office adjacent to the small room with the flicker fusion equipment.

"I need a minute. Susie had us up all night—another ear infection. I had to fill a prescription this morning. Something to look forward to when you have kids. If we're lucky, she'll outgrow them before she starts school."

"Poor kid." Richard adored the three-year-old who'd curl up next to him on the sofa to have a story read when he and Marty babysat.

"She'll survive. I guess we will too. Which reminds me. Can you babysit tomorrow, assuming Susie is okay?"

"Sure. I'd love it."

"You're invited to dinner—nothing fancy. We're meeting friends about 8:00. How soon do you leave for South Dakota?"

"Wednesday, probably. If you're satisfied with the data we have."

"If I need more, you'll be back. I'll look it over while you're gone, run a few statistical tests, see what we've got." As he talked, Seth pulled a book out of his army surplus jacket. "Ever read *Spoon River Anthology*?"

"Maybe, in high school, long ago. Can't say I really remember it. Why?"

"It's a collection of biographies in free verse of desperate, secret lives in a rural town. I thought of it when you told me about Don. You can keep my copy as long as you want. By the way, any more thoughts about buying an apartment building with the inheritance?"

"No point in discussing that until I know where I'll be next year." Richard had never expressed his fear to Seth that Marty might not marry him.

"Why wouldn't you stay here? Given your interests, Hopkins is good, but this faculty—including bio-psych—is excellent."

"I know. I had that great neuroanatomy course with Sperry last quarter. But I need financial help to complete a doctorate. I've used up my GI Bill."

"I don't know about fellowships, but you won't have any problems getting a job as a research assistant or associate. And Marty? Won't she be working?"

"I suspect she'll stay in school, get a doctorate—or a second masters."

By early afternoon, they had finished several runs. When Seth was ready to quit, Richard went to the animal lab to find Spence and take him through the routine. "Nothing difficult, but the rats have to be fed and watered every day. I appreciate this and promise to reciprocate."

"I'm here every day anyway looking after the cats. Want a beer later?"

"Gail invited me to dinner and I have a mountain of wash to do before. After dinner I'm heading to Clark and Clark for the book sale. I want something to read on the train. If you want to drop by there about 9:00, we can go to Jimmy's then or my place for a beer."

"Okay, see you later."

Dinner was good, but Richard left Gail's still hungry. She was generous in her invitations, yet stingy with her tiny servings of liver, potatoes, and peas. He knew they couldn't afford more than liver, lamb patties, or hamburger now, but once Bill had his MD, they'd do much better financially than Rich and his graduate school friends. Marty's acceptance of second or third or even fourth hand furniture and books from departing graduate students was definitely a positive quality for a woman married to an untenured professor.

Gail was reviewing the history of a crib she inherited from a friend—a crib that had already bedded six infants—when Bill, as eager as Richard to escape Gail's fixation, invited Richard to ride in their "new" pre-war Dodge coupe, a gift from Bill's mother. Under the streetlight Richard could not tell the color of the car, but he identified the make and model. "Hey, this is the car Bogart drove. In a movie with Lizabeth Scott. Do you remember the name of the movie?"

"*Dead Reckoning*, maybe. Not one of his best. Where should I drop you off?"

"Clark and Clark?"

"Okay."

Richard was thumbing through a copy of *Walden II* when Spence arrived. "Have you read this?" Richard held up the book as Spence approached.

"Yeah, haven't you?"

"No. Should I?"

"His ideal society is interesting. Not to be confused with Thoreau, of course. I don't think you'd want to live there. Good train reading, though." Leaving a bookstore was never easy for Richard, but Spence coaxed him into walking to Jimmy's for a beer.

On Saturday morning Richard ran subjects and advised Pete on building a bookcase in the psychology shop. When his potential afternoon subject failed to show, he stayed in the shop with Pete until another graduate student cut off part of his thumb on the circular saw. That night he wrote to Marty:

> At 3:00 Nick Pappas cut his hand on the circular saw. While he and Pete were wrapping a rag around it, I went over to turn off the saw. I

was not prepared to see about ½ inch of his thumb, whole fingernail and all. I was shaken. It looked so incongruous lying there—kind of artificial—but all too real with dirt under the nail and kind of alive and human with a life of its own. I don't think Nick knew it was so bad. He remained calm and, apparently, without pain. We took him to Billings where the medics decided it was bad enough for the operating room. Pete and I answered questions at the admitting office, then went grocery shopping and ate dinner here (liver, potatoes, peas, ice cream). We parted at 8:30.

I had barely started tackling applications when Rob Stone appeared at the door, wanting to talk. He's very troubled, doesn't know what he wants to do. I told him to think about leaving school and taking his chances with the draft. I did tell him he could stay here and study. In the end he spent the night—reading, but not studying—and was here when I got up at noon. After I showered and shaved, we went to Alexanders for breakfast. I just didn't have the *elan vital* to cook.

Honey, if I had to live without you, I'd seek a physically active, non-studying life. I couldn't make out any other way, because I can't concentrate. At this point I think it's a toss-up between whether your parents or I need you most. I wish I didn't feel so dependent on you, since you are not so strongly dependent on me. And there was no mail from you today. I guess the last letter I got was ahead of itself and should have arrived today. I hope you'll phone tomorrow. It costs less in the evening. And it's worth it—to me anyway. But it probably won't be forthcoming, and instead I shall sustain myself with thoughts of our approaching reunion. I'll probably leave here Wednesday. I'm fighting a losing battle, getting more and more lonely and more and more stagnant without you.

I love you so much, Bushel and a Peck
Rich

For two days he focused on completing chores and tying up loose ends.

Chapter Fifteen

Richard's Discovery

Ellen put down her *House Beautiful* magazine. "Who'd like coffee and cookies? Charles, there's also cheese and crackers."

"In a minute." Marty was fascinated by *The Snows of Kilimanjaro*, this tale of death that reflected Hemingway's tragic sense of life—shaped, she assumed, by his father's suicide and his war experiences. She wondered how women fit in. Catherine in *A Farewell to Arms* and Maria in *For Whom the Bell Tolls* were sympathetic characters, but not this one.

CB interrupted her thoughts. "Let's go snack."

"Okay." She got up and followed him into the kitchen.

"Marty, tell us more about Richard," Ellen said, holding out a plate of cookies. Cheddar and Danish bleu cheeses sat on a plate with crackers.

"He grew up in Trenton, NJ. Dad, you always asked me what my boyfriends' fathers did for a living. Rich's Dad is a wood pattern-maker. I'm pretty sure his parents are Republican."

CB sliced the cheddar. "Your Mom is probably more interested in their religion, but too polite to ask."

"I know they're not Catholic. Rich's father may sing in a Baptist choir."

"Is Rich Republican and Baptist like his parents?"

"No, Dad. But he had a good upbringing! And he's very smart. He will be a professor someday and like his job. That's most important."

They continued to talk about graduate school and jobs until almost midnight when CB stood up. "I think it's time to turn in."

Floating between sleep and wakefulness, Marty heard a phone ringing and someone moving around.

Ellen's voice brought her fully awake. "Marty, Mrs. Roberts just called. Grandma passed away."

Marty searched for the clothes she discarded earlier. Her feelings in disarray, she got into the back seat of the car behind her father. Grateful for the darkness, trembling, she crossed her arms, pulling her coat together. *Do calls about death always come at night?* She put her hand on her father's shoulder, "I'm so sorry, Dad."

Mrs. Roberts met them at the door and ushered them into the dimly lit room. CB approached his mother's bed and reached out to touch her.

"She's still warm," he whispered, as if to protect the other patients. Standing quietly, Marty shivered, awed in the presence of death.

When they returned home, Marty saw the Hemingway on the chair where she left it. Could she ever read *The Snows of Kilimanjaro* again without wondering who was about to die? She collapsed on the chair, her mind scrambled with images and thoughts of her grandmother. Without pausing, her parents said "Goodnight" and went upstairs, leaving her alone, to wonder at their calm acceptance of death. Her father must feel relief—and

Mom, too. But never to see his mother again, to talk to her? Soon she heard him snoring. *Grandma's death may be a "blessing," but why can he sleep while I'm agitated?* After awhile Marty went upstairs. *I might as well be sleepless in bed.*

Funeral arrangements were underway when Marty came downstairs the next morning. CB went to the funeral home while Ellen contacted relatives. CB's two brothers and sister would fly in that evening. Marty offered to call Liz.

"I'm sorry about Grandma's death. But I won't be expected, will I? I just saw her."

"No, Liz, you're off the hook. But you will miss the California relatives."

"I'll survive."

"I should get off the phone. I still have to call Rich."

Richard did not answer at his apartment, so Marty called the lab.

Spence answered, "He's here, Marty. Hang on."

"Marty, what a surprise. What's up?"

"Rich, Grandma died last night."

"I'm sorry. How are you?"

"Okay. This doesn't change anything. My relatives will be leaving before you get here, according to my mother. I can hardly wait to see you."

"Me too. Won't be long now. Give your folks my sympathy. Love ya."

Marty's sadness was modulated by recurrent thoughts about the convenient timing of her grandmother's death. Her father would be free now to come to Chicago without guilt, and she would not have to make a return trip at some later date for a funeral. *Thank God for small favors.*

Starting early in the day, friends and acquaintances came with food and flowers. Marty was amazed at how quickly word got around and people mobilized in a small town. Jessie brought muffins and word that the women from the church would serve dinner after the relatives arrived.

When Marty heard CB with his siblings in the front hall, she went to greet relatives she'd met only once when her family drove to California in the late '30s.

"Marty you were just a little tyke when we saw you last." Edward, the oldest, was the big brother her father always admired.

"I know. It's sad when relatives live so far apart." She sat on the sofa to watch and listen.

"Charles, much has changed, but the house feels the same." Ernest was younger than CB by a year or two. "Was this the room that had the old coal stove father loved to sit in front of?"

"He did love to watch the fire in that stove. We had it removed years ago when Liz was a baby, when we converted the house to a duplex."

"I remember Mother's china cabinet and the black walnut table." Margaret, younger than her brothers by several years, sat down next to Marty. "Do you still have the china Mother hand painted?"

"Yes, Ellen uses those dishes once in a while when we have company. Maybe they'll get used tonight."

Margaret looked intently at her brother. "Charles, where is Mother's diamond?"

"It's in a safe deposit box. Mother left that ring to Marty and the ring with the ruby and pearls to Liz. Her only granddaughters."

"What? I'm the only daughter." Margaret began to sniffle. "I can't believe Mother would do that to me."

Unaware of this legacy—surprised and sorry—Marty put her arms around her aunt. "Aunt Margaret, you can have the diamond."

"Marty, it was your grandmother's wish . . ." CB's stern voice left no room for debate.

Marty wanted to escape to the kitchen, but she stayed out of politeness, trying to comfort her distraught aunt, as the four discussed the disposal of their mother's property.

"Charlie, I'm sure that's Mother's marble top table."

"Yes, Margaret, you can ship it to California if you want."

"Where's the rest of her jewelry? She had nice things besides the rings."

"Ellen thought the three of you could sort that out. You know, Ed and Ernie may want to take something for their wives."

Ernie spoke up, "Thanks, Charles. Margaret, I know Dorothy would like something to remember Mother by."

Retreating to the kitchen at last, Marty wiped dishes as Ellen washed. "Mom, I can't believe what I'm hearing. They're less sad about their mother's death than worried about what they're going to get. I swear I will never be so petty. I'll never behave that way with Liz. Was it like that in your family?"

"No, Marty, there was nothing to fight over."

As the day of Richard's arrival approached, Marty's guilt and anxiety intensified. What should she tell Richard about Wallly? If she avoided the issue and one of her parents inadvertently said something, how could she explain her silence? By telling him, she would eliminate her fear of his finding out, but not her fear of his reaction. She could not face the loss of his love, his trust. If only she had asked Wally where he got his money for the voyage on their first date, she wouldn't have gone to the motel.

On the day of Richard's arrival, however, Marty's eagerness to see him overshadowed everything and bolstered her optimism. *All will be okay. Richard will forgive.* She welcomed her father's offer to drive her to the C&NW train station. Why should he trust her to drive his relatively new Pontiac?

As CB parked behind the station, Marty heard the train whistle—evocative of her early trips to Chicago on the Dakota

400 and the nights she read Thomas Wolfe under the covers with a flashlight.

Kissing Richard with her father standing nearby would embarrass everyone, so she asked CB to stay in the car. She walked quickly along the platform, past several baggage carts toward the train and the nearest passenger car. Fidgeting, expectant, Marty watched the conductor step down from the train and extend a hand to a middle-aged woman before Richard emerged, bag in hand. Marty ran toward him and threw her arms around his neck. His kiss was sweet.

"God, it's great to see you. This separation has been torture. How are you?"

"Better, especially now that you're here. And we can leave soon." Marty smiled, happier than she'd been in weeks. They walked to the car in matching strides, arm in arm. CB met them partway, shook hands with Richard and took his bag to put in the trunk.

"CB, I was sorry to hear about your mother. This is a tough time. I appreciate your inviting me." Richard opened the door to the back seat.

"We're glad to have you. Marty says it's your first trip to South Dakota."

"Yes, I've been looking forward to it."

"Rich, sit in front. There's room for three." Marty shifted so he could squeeze in. "Stay alert now. We're about to pass the tallest building in town—seven stories—and kitty-corner is the post office, where Dad worked years ago. And that little brick building used to be a hospital. Liz and I were both born there."

"Hey, slow down. I can't take it all in at once."

Beyond his voice, she felt his arm around her shoulder, his hand squeezing her upper arm. For the moment she was truly happy.

Marty ushered Richard into the kitchen.

"Welcome, Richard, it's so nice you could come visit." Ellen brushed her floury hands across her apron and held out a hand.

"Thanks, Mrs. Black. That home-cooked food smells wonderful."

"Dinner's almost ready. Wash up."

After dinner, Richard and Marty did the dishes. So they could be alone, Marty plotted a walk to the neighborhood grocery store for cigarettes and anything Ellen might need. CB, missing the point, offered to drive.

"Thanks, Dad, but we'd like to exercise. Rich has been sitting all day." Outside, they embraced and kissed.

"Maybe that will keep me warm. It's freezing," Richard said.

"Forget the calendar. Spring rarely gets here before April." Marty put her arm through his and pressed her head against him. "It's so wonderful to be with you."

At the Fair Deal Grocery Marty introduced Richard to a brother of Anna Otis, the childhood friend from kindergarten, who lived in Florida now with her husband and one or two children.

"It's a family business," Marty explained to Richard later. "When we were growing up, Anna, her sister, and two brothers worked in the store with their father. I rarely saw Mrs. Otis. They lived in a nice house next to the store and had a German maid. She did most of the cooking, but I think it was Mrs. Otis who made great pastries on Greek holidays. No one else I knew had a live-in maid in the '30s. But what impressed me most was the candy Anna always had. No one seemed to care how much she took out of the display cases in the store."

"Are you still in touch with her?" Richard asked.

"I used to send Christmas cards but she hardly ever did. Sad, isn't it. We did so much growing up together: walked to and from school, rode bikes, played with paper dolls, went ice skating." An image of Wally skating flashed in her mind. "We played Monopoly and card games, and spent hours arguing politics. I must have been the only Republican in my class. In those days everyone—you, too, I'm sure—thought Roosevelt was the greatest. We also talked about boys—even in grade school. As I remember, we each had a hierarchy. The same three or four boys would alternate from favorite to second favorite, etc., on a weekly basis. I don't remember how we decided, although being 'cute' was important."

As they approached her house, Marty reached for Richard's hand. "Thanks for coming. Sorry we can't be together tonight."

"That's okay. Seeing you is good enough."

Although CB still needed to talk about Don's death, he was less emotional, less intense than in previous weeks. But Richard was a new sounding board, a fresh opportunity to revisit the evidence, possibly hear a new perspective, and CB held him captive whenever he could. During dinner on Richard's second night, CB reported on his latest conversation with the investigator. "To date he's checked about half the motel registrations."

"He's looking for suspicious customers who were in town that week?" Richard asked.

"Yes. He's also checking car registrations."

Marty, flustered at the mention of the car, lost the train of the conversation—until CB startled her with a question. "Was that the day you went skating with Wally?"

Instinctively, Marty glanced at Richard. In the same instant he looked at her—questioning. "No," she answered, not certain which day her father referred to. "I don't know."

As they helped Ellen clear off the table, Richard asked Marty to go for a walk.

"It's awfully cold and windy out."

"You two should take the car and go to a movie or have a drink at the Pheasant Lounge. Ellen and I aren't going anywhere tonight."

"I'd like to see more of your town, Marty. Okay?"

"Sure." *Might as well face it now.* She saw Richard take the keys from her father as she turned toward the front hall and her coat.

"You're navigator, Marty. Where do I go?" Richard had started the car and was looking at her.

"How about a movie? I don't know what's playing now that the Abbot and Costello movie is gone. We could drive by and look."

"No. I'd like to talk. As much as I like your parents, it's nice to be alone."

"Okay, let's drive downtown? It's not Rush Street, but we can take our pick of a couple of bars. Not much else to do, especially on a week night." They were on Dakota Avenue in minutes, driving slowly down the quiet, broad, main street, reading colorful neon signs that accentuated the dreariness of a windy, March evening in this flat, prairie town. "Remind you of a movie set for a Western?" Marty tried to see her hometown through his eyes.

"No. It reminds me of *It's A Wonderful Life*. It simplifies decision making. There aren't many places to stop for a drink. My first impression is that things are spread out. Streets are wide; lots are big. Nothing feels crowded. Where do I go?"

"Turn left here and go a block." She wanted to avoid the Pheasant Lounge where someone might remember seeing her with Wally. "This bar is small, but it's a weeknight. I don't think it'll be crowded. We'll be able to get a booth."

Two men she did not recognize sat at the bar. Richard led her to the booth farthest away and went back to the bar to order drinks. She lit a cigarette and waited.

"Marty, all those wet letters in your apartment were from Wally." He put a Scotch and water in front of her.

"I told you about him, the closest thing I had to a boyfriend in high school. We only had a couple of real dates. We'd end up together at parties and after games, occasionally. Kid stuff. Young kid stuff."

"Most of those letters were sent from Berkeley."

"I think I only saw him once after college."

"Why did you save his letters?"

"I'm a letter-saver. If you look in my parents' attic, you'll find others I've saved."

"Were you in love with him?"

Maybe . . . "No!"

"You went skating with him."

"He was in town briefly. We had dinner one night and I said I'd like to skate again. The next day he found old skates in his parents' basement and called me."

"What was it like—seeing him again?"

"Richard, stop it—or I'll start asking about your high school friends and the girls you dated in the army. How about Japanese women?"

"What do you want to know?"

"Everything. Nothing. It's your past. Tell me what *you* want."

"Marty, I'm asking about a recent meeting with an old boyfriend whose letters you've saved. I haven't looked at another woman since we started seeing each other."

"Fine. There's a long story and I'm not sure this is the time or place to get into it."

"Why not? We have the entire evening."

"And you won't stop bugging me?"

"Probably not."

Marty tried to avoid his gaze. As she consumed a second Scotch and water, she told her story, stressing her need to establish Wally's guilt or innocence. Richard listened quietly until she mentioned the motel room.

"You went to a motel?"

"We had to leave the restaurant, and I had to know where he got his money."

"And you *had* to go to a motel! Did you ever ask him directly?"

"Yes, I finally got the answer."

"Okay. This is the tough one, but I need to know the truth. Marty, did you sleep with him?"

Marty's eyelids twitched as she looked away, her hand reached for her drink. "Yes."

"Let's get out of here." He got up and walked to the bar to pay the bill.

Ashamed, Marty hurried after him, her stomach churning. Outside, she grabbed his arm. "Rich, I'm sorry. I didn't mean to hurt you. I only wanted information. If you'd lived through those weeks with my father, you'd understand. I probably was a little crazy. Even now, the money is still missing."

"You were willing to sleep with him for information." Richard passed the car and continued walking.

"Where are you going?"

"I don't know. Not back to your house."

"Okay, let's walk. Yell at me; hit me. Do whatever will make you feel better."

"What I'd like to do is get out of here." They walked in silence for blocks. Finally, Richard stopped. "Marty, do you love him?"

"No!"

"That's hard to believe."

"He's just an old friend."

Several silent blocks later, Richard stopped again. "I don't know where I am, but if you can find the car, I'm ready to go to your place."

Returning to the car, Marty finally got up enough courage to ask, "Rich, will you ever forgive me?"

"I don't know."

Richard did not speak again until they were in the car. "Marty, I can't stay. I'm going to your house, get my things, and leave on the first train back to Chicago."

"Please Rich, can't we work this out? I love you. I made a terrible mistake. I'm sorry. Forgive me," she pleaded.

"I can't."

"In one of your letters, you said you'd love me forever no matter what."

"If I didn't love you, your betrayal wouldn't hurt so much."

"Then stay! I'll make it up to you somehow."

"I wish you could undo it, but you can't." Richard parked in front of the house. "I'll be right back with my bag. You *will* drive me to the station?"

"Please, Rich." Marty was crying softly. "Try not to wake up my parents." She waited, feeling like her whole future was unraveling.

On the way to the station Richard said, "Marty, please apologize to your parents for me. Tell them whatever you want about my leaving."

She didn't know what to say. Nothing would change his mind now.

He parked behind the station and turned to her before he got out of the car. "I don't want you to come into the station. This is hard enough." In a second he vanished.

For several minutes she sat staring at the spot where he disappeared into the darkness. Her hands shook as she turned on the engine. She felt as if she'd taken a body blow. She tried to concentrate on driving, but she couldn't escape the pain reflected in Richard's eyes when he left her. His anguish and now hers touched a deep chord of her being. Her betrayal seemed reprehensible, her disregard for his feelings, her lack of empathy. She deserved to lose him. She realized the prelude of her life had modulated from a simple, sweet harmony to dissonance through her own recklessness. Did she finally know what she wanted now that it was too late?

Her hands were still shaking when she parked the car and walked up to the front door. Inside, she passed through the hallway into the living room and stood before the window that looked out onto the front yard, still covered with snow that glistened under the streetlight. She fumbled for a cigarette in her purse. *I should quit smoking.*

Epilogue

South Dakota, 1998

Lying in bed in the room adjacent to Don's old bedroom, Marty listened to the wind and the voices, and saw the snow building up on the ledge outside the window. *Perfect weather for revisiting February, 1953 or for staying in bed. No time for the latter.* She had set the thermostat for 65 degrees, but it felt much colder as she pulled on a pair of jeans and Rich's old black turtleneck, rolling up the long sleeves as she rushed downstairs.

She admired the tall, antique, four-legged stove—the Cadillac of the '20s, the stove Don's mother bought—while she made coffee in Ellen's percolator on one of the burners she lit with a wooden match. She thought of this as Don's house, even though Ellen lived here for decades until her death in November. At the funeral Liz had agreed to return here in February to put the house on the market after they disposed of its contents.

Before Liz's arrival, Marty hoped to read the correspondence she exchanged with Richard the winter Don and her grandmother died—letters she saved with the yellowed newspaper clippings of the death. Over the years she'd been too busy to reflect much on her past or reread these letters she'd brought now from home. Armed with coffee, she settled in the living room on the old horsehair sofa, long since covered with a tapestry-like fabric. At first she tried to read the letters in sequence, but soon she put her letters aside and concentrated on Richard's. His voice seemed as clear as ever, his image, sharp, as he leaned toward her in the booth, took her hand. *Let's get married.* She'd never forget his serious blue eyes, his unruly hair, and his broad shoulders in the black turtleneck.

Other memories, long submerged in some dark recess of her mind, also came to light. And a likely explanation for the disappearance of Don's money—a new theory she'd try out on Liz.

Mid-afternoon, Marty finished reading the last of Richard's letters and began an inventory of Ellen's desk drawers. When Liz called from the airport, Marty offered to pick her up, but Liz decided a cab would be faster. Forty-five minutes later she rang the doorbell. Marty greeted her with a quick hug and directed her into the den. One look at the mess—papers and cartons scattered about—and Liz collapsed on a chair.

"God! This will take forever unless we burn the place down."

"It's not that bad. We dispose of the irrelevant papers, decide what we want to keep, and then hire an auctioneer to sell the rest."

"That's *all*? I don't want anything, do you?"

"Yes, I like old things that remind me of Mom and Dad. And Grandma too. Some things, like a drawer full of hats I found upstairs—hats Mom wore in the '30s—we should probably donate to a theatre group."

That night over dinner at the local chicken shack they discussed in detail the disposition of their mother's property. As they talked about the sale of the house, Marty said, "Remember how tense it got before Dad decided to move into Don's house?"

"Not really," Liz said, salting her French fries.

"That's right, you left for Chicago soon after the funeral. You know, I really resented your leaving right after the funeral— one reason I had a hard time talking to you after I got back to Chicago. You were so self-centered then. Have you thought much about Don's death since 1953?"

"Marty, I'm sorry about returning to Chicago so soon. I didn't know it bothered you."

"Of course not. You were oblivious. Really."

"Sorry again. I thought both of us believed it was suicide. Didn't you?"

"Well, the missing money raised doubts. I really didn't think much about it, though, after I got back to Chicago. Years later, after I retired, I began reflecting more on my life and wondering again about Don's death and the missing money."

"Did that private investigator ever discover anything?"

"No. And Dad searched the house for months. Remember? He found those gold coins in the basement. Nothing else. Interested in dessert?"

"No. I have to watch my waistline. I already ate most of the French fries. Do you think Dad was ever okay about living in Don's house?"

"He seemed to be, but he kept a pistol in a desk drawer. He didn't own a pistol before they moved there. Liz, I just reread the newspaper clippings about Don's death and the letters Rich and I exchanged that winter. I have a new theory about what happened."

"Really? Tell me."

"I think Don gave the money to Meyer. Maybe to deliver to someone. Obviously, Don didn't leave the house to dispose of it and the money was not in the house. And there was no evidence of someone in the house demanding payment."

"But no one came forward. We did wonder if a woman got the money somehow and was too embarrassed to admit it."

"Right. I think it's more likely that Don told Meyer to keep the money."

"But why? Meyer was in the will."

"Maybe he wanted to give Meyer more for being an especially good, long-time employee. It was too late for a codicil to the will and he didn't want his other employees to know anyway."

"Under the circumstance, wouldn't Meyer have told?"

"Not if he was sworn to secrecy. If he'd been asked to deliver it to someone . . . maybe. Otherwise, no. To keep peace in the store, to prevent hurt feelings."

"Well, it's an interesting theory. Why didn't we consider it, or something like it, at the time?"

"We assumed the money would show up. We never gave up totally on that theory. And we trusted Meyer's story about giving the money to Don and returning to the store."

"Your theory does make sense. But does it matter any more, Marty? Everyone involved is dead—except us."

"You're right. I just couldn't stop wondering."

The next morning, fortified with coffee, they worked together in the den.

"Save anything relevant to Mom's income tax in this carton."

"Liz, how about these personal letters?"

"Toss, I guess. Unless you want to read them."

"I may look at them later. You know me. I'm a letter saver."

"Speaking of personal, Marty, I never did know why Rich came back to Chicago without you that winter."

"My fault. I had a couple of dates with Wally."

"Couple of dates?"

"Well, it got serious, briefly."

"Serious?" Liz looked intently at her sister. "You slept with him! I'm surprised at you, Marty." She shook her head. "Luckily, Rich got over it quickly. You were married by the end of the summer."

"It didn't seem quick to me. I was miserable for a long time after he walked out that night. Mom and Dad were okay. Didn't ask many questions. Going back to Chicago was awful. I couldn't concentrate. I felt lost all spring quarter. Dr. Martin kept me busy at work and that helped some."

"Why didn't you call me?"

"Liz, what could you do? Anyway, we didn't have that kind of relationship. I didn't even talk to Gail. She was totally involved with her pregnancy and then the new baby. I had a lot of private soul-searching to do."

"And you suffered silently. I know. It's a family trait. Well, how did you and Rich get back together?"

"A few months later I was in Jimmy's—my first date after our breakup. Richard was there with a cute blonde. We didn't speak, but we kept looking at each other. The next day he called and asked me to dinner at Alexanders."

"And you made up. He forgave you."

"Yes, but it wasn't automatic. Convincing him I really loved him didn't happen overnight. He said it might take a long time before he could trust me again. I understood. I said I could live with it. I promised I would never, ever betray him again, never take his love for granted. I still find it hard to use that word—betrayal."

"Because you didn't feel you'd betrayed him?"

"We weren't engaged. I tried not to think about Rich when I was with Wally. Afterwards, I couldn't accept and admit I'd done something so awful. Not at first. What's worse than betrayal?"

"Well it worked out . . . you got married."

"Right! I beat you by a few years."

"In more ways than one. My marriage was a disaster. Yours worked. You were a good team."

"You didn't find the right guy."

"No. Marriage wasn't for me. I should have stuck to my original belief. Too bad Rich died so young."

"Yes. At least the boys were grown and I had a career to keep me occupied—thanks partly to the inheritance."

"Marty, what became of Wally?"

"I learned at a class reunion that he was killed in a brawl in Morocco. Stabbed to death. I never saw or heard from him after our brief encounter. So many deaths. Gail died at 41 of brain cancer. Jessie almost made it to 100. Mom and Jessie, the last of their generation."

"This is getting morbid. You and I are still alive and healthy."

"Let's take a break. Eat something."

"Okay. As soon as I dump these political brochures."

"Mom never stopped being a Republican. Loyal to the end."

Liz opened the refrigerator door. "What's to eat?"

"I bought a few things yesterday. How about cold cereal or a peanut butter sandwich?"

"Peanut butter? How regressive can you get?"

"I've always loved peanut butter. I guess I have been regressive in my recent preoccupation with the past. Tonight is actually the 45th anniversary of Don's death."

"I'm amazed you remembered the exact date. All I remembered was the season, because there'd been a blizzard." Liz poured milk on a bowl of cereal.

"Any interest in driving by the house we grew up in or the high school or any other place?"

"Let's get through the paper sorting before we drive around town. And how about a short recital on the old Gilbranson?"

"Sorry, it's badly out of tune. I tried playing yesterday, but I couldn't stand it."

After lunch, Liz and Marty returned to the den to clean out the roll top desk and a filing cabinet, reminiscing about their childhood as they uncovered relevant papers. When they'd gone through all but a stack of legal documents, they carried the cartons of discarded papers to the back hall to be disposed of with the trash.

"Marty, we're almost through in here. Why don't I finish with this legal stuff and you look into the desk and the cabinets below the built-in bookcases in the living room? I'm not sure what Mom kept in there."

"Good idea." In the living room Marty looked at the shelves filled with Modern Library editions she and Liz acquired in college, and leather-bound books their parents and grandparents collected much earlier. "Liz, we have tons of books here."

"I know," Liz yelled from the den. "Let's tackle them together tonight."

Marty opened the slant top desk. Inside she found a pen and pencils, an address book and a box of stationary. She reached for the only mail she saw—a single envelope that protruded from one compartment addressed to "Marty and Liz" in Ellen's handwriting. Her heart began to pound.

Dear Marty and Liz,

This is hard, but I feel it must be done before I'm too old and feeble. I hope you'll understand.

You know that after Nellie's death, Don often ate dinner at our house. One night when he was supposed to eat here, he called to say he had an emergency at the house and he had to meet there with an electrician. So I took dinner over to him. He was very depressed—not about the electrical problem. He was terribly lonely, almost in tears at one point. I tried to cheer him up. With your father out of town so much, I was lonely too. What began as two friends comforting each other turned into a very brief affair.

Somehow, Bob Meyer found out and started demanding money. I don't think Don minded the money so much, but Meyer was getting more and more greedy. Don just couldn't take it any longer and he didn't want our family hurt by scandal. Please forgive me.

I love you both,
Mom

Marty sat down, trying to take it in, her hands shaking now. *I can't believe it. Poor Mom. To live with that all these years.* She read the note again and again before she called to Liz, trying to control her voice.

"Liz, come here. I've got something important to show you."

"Don't get hysterical, Marty. Let's have a drink before dinner. It's almost time. I hope you bought liquor when you picked up the cartons yesterday."

Clutching the note, Marty walked into the kitchen.

Liz appeared in the doorway. "What is it?"

"Read this—a letter from Mom that settles the mystery. I was on the right track, but neither of us could have imagined this."

"Your Meyer theory sounded reasonable last night." Liz reached for the note Marty held out. A few seconds later she looked up, shook her head. "You're right. I would never have guessed. So out of character for both Mom and Don."

"Especially Mom. I thought I knew her. Liz, you'll have to make us drinks, my hands are still shaking."

"No problem, the ingredients are here for Martinis. I thought I knew Mom too. Really makes you hate Meyer, the bastard. We *sure* didn't know him. To think we just accepted his story. Why?"

"We trusted him because we thought Don trusted him. We believed he gave the money to Don and went back to the store as he said. When no one came forward, we assumed it was in the house. People were more trusting in those days. It never occurred to us he might not be telling the whole truth."

"Or that Mom would have an affair." Liz handed Marty a Martini.

"That's the hard part. She always seemed so puritanical or Victorian."

"I forgive her."

"So do I. Aren't you a little angry that she betrayed Dad and let us speculate *ad nausea* about the money?"

"Marty, I'm just glad the mystery is solved. Let's drink a toast to Mom, Dad, and Don and that generation. They did a lot for us. Celebrate their lives."

"Okay. I'll drink a toast to you too. You've been a good sister. I don't even resent your overshadowing me most of my life." Marty laughed as she raised her glass.

"Why should you? Mom and Dad loved you most because you were the most caring. You were more daughterly than me. You stayed when Don and Grandma died. You visited many times over the years. I was too busy."

"You know, I had to become a parent to understand that you weren't favored. First born are treated differently but it doesn't mean they are more loved."

"Marty, you're the one who had it all—marriage, kids and career."

"I was lucky. I don't regret marrying Richard and raising two sons, but my career in psychology didn't compare with yours in law."

"I'm sorry Dad didn't live long enough to see me succeed in his favored profession. At least he knew I made it to law school."

"Liz, he knew you'd be a success."

"Maybe. In the long run, though, you probably helped more people than I ever did."

"That's hard to measure."

"When it comes to Dad—and Mom too—they loved their grandsons more than anything, so you were the big achiever. No career—even in politics—could match up to that legacy."

"Hey, we have reasons for several toasts."

When Marty heard the mantel clock strike twelve, she put down the Marquis novel she'd started and turned off the light on the chest next to her bed. She decided she'd better get some sleep, to be prepared for whatever they might find next. *Life is so unpredictable,* she thought. *Don's death should have taught me that. Still, life is a wonderful gift . . . if you can accept the surprises, hang on to the good memories, and appreciate the simple things.* She fell asleep planning to have the kids and their families for dinner as soon as she got home.

The End